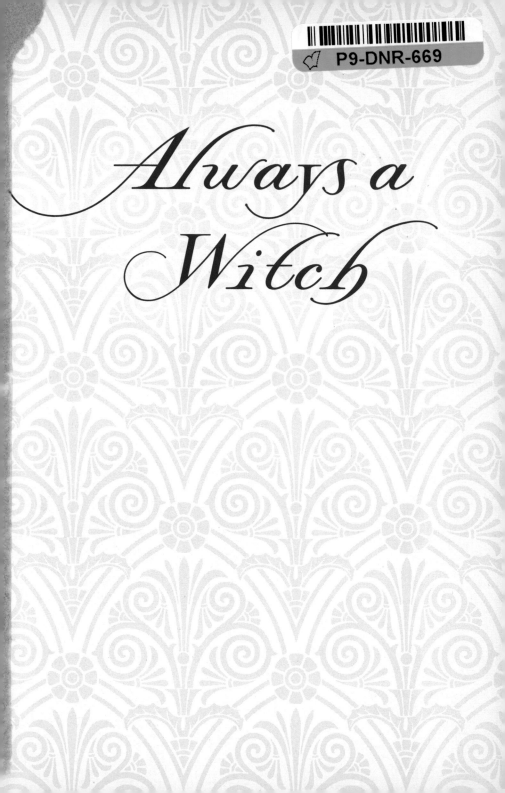

Always a Witch

Always a Witch

by CAROLYN MACCULLOUGH

CLARION BOOKS

HOUGHTON MIFFLIN HARCOURT
Boston New York
2011

For Frankie and Ella

Clarion Books
215 Park Avenue South
New York, New York 10003

Copyright © 2011 by Carolyn MacCullough

Clarion Books is an imprint of
Houghton Mifflin Harcourt Publishing Company.

www.hmhbooks.com

The text was set in Horley Old Style MT Light.

Library of Congress Cataloging-in-Publication Data

MacCullough, Carolyn.
Always a witch / by Carolyn MacCullough.
p. cm.
Summary: Haunted by her grandmother's prophecy that she will
soon be forced to make a terrible decision, witch Tamsin Greene risks
everything to travel back in time to 1887 New York to confront the
enemy that wants to destroy her family.
ISBN 978-0-547-22485-5
[1. Witches—Fiction. 2. Time travel—Fiction. 3. Ability—Fiction. 4. Good and evil—
Fiction. 5. New York (N.Y.)—History—1865-1898—Fiction.] I. Title.
PZ7.M1389Al 2011
[Fic]—dc22
2011008148

Manufactured in the United States of America
DOC 10 9 8 7 6 5 4 3 2 1
4500297831

ACKNOWLEDGMENTS

A big thank-you to my family and friends for putting up with me during the writing of this book. Thank you to Alyssa Eisner Henkin, whose enthusiasm and guidance on this project was very much appreciated! And finally, I was lucky enough to have not one but two very wonderful editors for this book. Thank you to Jennifer Wingertzahn for getting the ball rolling, and thank you to Daniel Nayeri, who picked up so seamlessly where she left off.

Always a Witch

PROLOGUE

I WAS BORN ON THE NIGHT of Samhain. Others might call it Halloween. Born into a family of witches who all carry various Talents. Others might call it magic.

Except for me.

I alone in my family seemed to have no Talent. No gift to shape me or to grant me a place in my family's circle around the altar to the four elements. All I had was the prophecy that my grandmother made to my mother in the first hour of my life. *"Your daughter will be one of the most powerful we have ever seen in this family. She will be a beacon for us all."*

And then for reasons still unknown, my grandmother spent the next seventeen years making sure I *doubted* that prophecy at every turn. It took the return of an old family enemy, two episodes of time travel, and one very dangerous love spell that nearly killed my sister before I learned three things. First, I can stop anyone from using their Talent to harm me. Second, I can absorb a person's Talent if they attempt to use it against me three times. Third, I apparently have a choice ahead of me. A choice that will explain the mysterious workings of my grandmother's mind and why she raised me in complete denial of my Talent. A choice that's vaguely hinted at in my family's book. A choice that will fulfill the prophecy my grandmother made all those years ago.

Or destroy my family forever.

A choice that will be so terrible to contemplate that I'd just rather not encounter it at all.

ONE

"I LOOK AWFUL," I SAY, staring at myself in front of the dressing room mirror. The dress I have just struggled into hangs like a shapeless tent down to my ankles. Okay, actually, it clings to the top half of me a little too tightly before suddenly dropping off into the aforementioned shapeless tent. And it's gray. Not silver, not opalescent mist, as the tag promises. Gray. Concrete gray.

My best friend, Agatha, scrunches her eyebrows together over her bright green eyeglasses as she examines me from all angles. "You do look awful. Perfectly awful, in fact," she finally confirms.

I stick my tongue out at her. Agatha loves the word *perfectly* just a little too much. "Yeah, well, that was probably Rowena's intention all along," I mutter, struggling to find the zipper. The overhead lights of the narrow boutique are suddenly too hot and glaring.

"Here," Agatha says, and with swift fingers she yanks the zipper down.

With a sigh of relief, I slip back into my jeans and flowered T-shirt, then step into my fringed wedges that I found in my favorite thrift store last week. I can't resist them, even though my ankles start to throb after more than five minutes of wearing them.

"Why can't you wear your rose dress?" Agatha asks again as she arranges the hated gray tent back on its hanger. Rowena had pronounced it "ethereal" when she had been in the city a few weeks earlier and had left me three messages on my cell to come to the store "at once." However, I never picked up the phone. Caller ID is one of the best inventions out there.

"Because Rowena wants silver. And what Rowena wants, Rowena gets."

"Bridezilla, huh?"

"She gives new meaning to that term." I refasten my pink barrettes to the side of my head; useless, I know, since they'll be falling out in about three minutes. My curly hair defies all devices invented to contain it.

"Too bad," Agatha says as we exit the dressing room. "That rose dress is *so* pretty and you never get to wear it."

"Yeah," I say, keeping my expression noncommittal, while inwardly feeling the familiar pang. Oh, how I wish I could tell Agatha that I already did wear it. I wore it when Gabriel and I Traveled back to 1939 to a garden party in my family's mansion on Washington Square Park in New York City. But if I told her that, I'd have to tell her who I really am. What I really am. And the truth is, I don't know who or what I really am. For most of my life I thought I was ordinary. The black sheep who got stuck in a very *extra*ordinary family. Not until I left my hometown of Hedgerow and came to boarding school in Manhattan did I learn not to mind that so much. For the first time in my life, I was surrounded by people who had no idea that just enough powdered mandrake root mixed with wine can make a man want to kiss you. But too much can make that same man want to kill you. It felt good to be among people who thought I was just like them. It felt normal. *I* felt normal. I felt like one of them.

And now that feeling is gone. And I can't decide if I'm happy or sad about that.

I gaze at Agatha for a moment and contemplate how to tell her that I don't really have a hippie crunchy granola kind of family, as she likes to think. Instead, I have a family of witches who actively practice their Talents but who still manage to live relatively obscure lives. I have a mother and grandmother who offer love spells, sleep spells, and spells for luck, good fortune, and health to the town residents who come knocking on the back door after night falls when they can't be seen by their neighbors. I have a father who controls the weather. A sister who can compel anyone to do anything just by mesmerizing them with the sound of her voice. My grandmother's sister who can freeze someone where he stands just by touching his forehead. A boyfriend who can find anything and anyone that's missing. A whole bunch of other people I've been taught to call "uncle" or "aunt" or "cousin" who are all Talented in one way or another.

If I told Agatha any of that, she'd look at me like I was speaking in tongues. If I showed her that I could shoot fire from my hands or freeze people into statues with one tap of my finger, she'd think I was a freakshow.

Or worse, she'd be afraid of me.

Agatha's one of the first and relatively few people who made me feel normal in my life. Back when I thought I didn't have a Talent at all, when I first came to boarding school in Manhattan, it was okay omitting certain things about my family life. It was okay to blur the line between the truth and a lie. But now that I've discovered I do have a Talent after all, it feels harder.

"So what are you going to do?" Agatha asks, breaking into my headlong rush of thoughts.

"What?" I blink at her until she flourishes the dress through the air. "Oh. I'm not buying that thing!"

The saleslady who has been hovering around the dressing room apparently overhears me. She takes the dress back from Agatha, stroking it like she's afraid its feelings just got hurt. Her long pink nose twitches once, reinforcing my initial impression of a rabbit. "Well," she says, her tone frosted over. "Your sister did say that was the one she wanted. She specifically asked me to put it aside for you even though it's *really* not our policy to do that here. Not for more than twenty-four hours and it's been *three* weeks already." The saleslady blinks a little as if suddenly wondering *why* she did break store policy.

I try not to roll my eyes. Apparently Rowena has won over yet another heart. People seem to want to throw themselves in front of speeding buses for Rowena. Part of her Talent and all. Not that she ever would abuse that. Oh, no.

"You know, she is the bride, after all. It's really *her* day," she says.

"No kidding," I reply sweetly. "She's been reminding us all of that for three months now."

"Still," the saleslady says, fluttering the hem at me. "I'm sure it looked lovely on you. Perhaps if you put on a bit more rouge and—"

The doorbell chimes softly and I look up to see Gabriel stepping into the store. Okay, I know it's lame, but my heart still does this weird fluttery thing sometimes when I see him. When the afternoon sunlight is hitting his cheekbones the way it is right now. When he smiles at me—that smile that makes me feel safe and not so safe at the same time. When he gives me that look that spells out, *I know you, Tamsin Greene. I know exactly who you are.*

Thankfully, someone does.

I smile back and manage to pull my gaze away long enough to shake my head at the saleslady. "I'll tell her it didn't fit me."

"Yeah, she was bursting out of it anyway," Agatha adds in helpfully. She makes a motion toward my chest.

"Really?" Gabriel says, interest streaking through his voice. "And that's a bad thing?"

Agatha bobs her head up and down. "You should have seen how—"

I clear my throat loudly. "*Okay*, thanks, everyone, but I think—"

Just then the door opens again and another woman shoulders past Gabriel, a look of desperation on her face. She swings a little black purse by a tasseled cord and I notice Gabriel take a step back to avoid getting hit in the jaw. "Do you have the new Dolce Vita dress in purple? It has to be purple. I've looked everywhere!"

Instantly, the saleslady's face assumes an expression of sorrow. "No," she whispers, her gaze wandering to a spot above the woman's shoulder as if eye contact is too much to bear during this difficult moment. "I'm so sorry. We only carry the Dolce Baci line."

"Oh!" the woman gives a muffled little shriek. "No one has this dress and I have to have—"

"Try Lily Lucile on Spring Street," Gabriel says helpfully. "They're carrying it. The purple one that you want."

A small silence fills the room as all eyes land on Gabriel. He turns his palms skyward, lifts his shoulders in a shrug. "Don't ask me how I know that," he murmurs.

And then, "Ah, Tam, I'll wait outside for you," he says, and ducks out.

Dusk is falling by the time Gabriel's front tires hit all the usual potholes of my family's driveway. The house is blazing with light and smoke tinges the air from tonight's bonfire, which I know is already burning behind the house. A small clump of my younger cousins chase each other across the snow-dusted meadow into the darkening woods beyond the house and fields.

"How pastoral," Gabriel says, grinning sideways at me.

"Yeah, until you look closer," I say, grinning back and leaning toward him. My seatbelt presses into my hip and I fumble to undo it, then decide not to bother.

Just then the air is split open. "Mother! I said I wanted peonies, not posies. Posies are ridiculous in winter. Who ever heard of a bride carrying posies anyway?"

Gabriel turns his head. "Are those Rowena's dulcet tones that I hear?"

I shift back into my seat just as my sister storms around the side of the yard, heading toward the house. The porch door opens and my mother steps out. She takes one look at my sister's face, then another look at my father, who is trailing Rowena, a bunch of yellow flowers drooping in his hand.

"Mother," Rowena yells again. "You need to explain something very important to my father." She flings one arm back to identify our father as if our mother is unclear on just who this man might be. "You need to tell him that I am getting married in three days. Three days and . . . *Mother!*"

I grin. The porch door remains closed, but mid-diatribe, my mother has simply vanished. No doubt she's zoomed into another part of the house at her usual lightning speed. Rowena skids to a stop, and for once her flaxen hair has escaped from its perfect chignon. She whirls around and looks at my father, who shrugs and begins slowly backing up toward his greenhouse, probably wishing right about now that he also possessed my mother's Talent of moving at warp speed. Then Rowena pivots again, her gaze narrowing in on Gabriel's car.

"Tamsin," she calls, her voice imperious as she starts down the driveway.

I sink down the length of my seat and begin picking at a tuft of foam that protrudes from a rip in the upholstery.

"Piece of advice?" Gabriel offers, his eyes tracking Rowena's progress toward us. "Don't tell her you didn't buy the dress."

As we step into the kitchen, carrying our bags, my mother, who is standing at the counter, looks up with a startled expression. "Tamsin," she says, her voice vibrating with relief. "And Gabriel," she adds, and offers us both a smile before turning back to the heap of glittering silverware that's piled on the counter. "You're here." She examines two butter knives, and then suddenly raises her head again like a hunted animal to glance behind us. "Where's Rowena?" she whispers.

"I froze her," I say, setting down my backpack and stretching my arms to the ceiling. "She makes a great statue in the garden."

Gabriel snorts and ducks his head into the open refrigerator as the knives slip from my mother's grasp and crash back on the pile of silverware. "You did?" she asks, a note of hope throbbing through her voice. Clearing her throat, she tries again. "I mean, you did what? You can't just freeze your sister."

I shrug. "It'll wear off. In a week or two. Is there anything to eat here?" I ask, and bump Gabriel with my hip as I join him at the fridge. We spend a few seconds in a shoving match as cold air billows in our faces.

My mother makes a noise like a teakettle coming to boil. "Tamsin—"

"Relax, Mom. I'm kidding," I say, stepping back, ending the fridge war. "She's chewing Aunt Linnie's ear off. Something about the tablecloths not being the right shade of cream and how Aunt Linnie has to dye them again. Or the world will come to an end."

"Is this all wedding food?" Gabriel asks, and I peer over his shoulder at the rows and rows of little iced cakes.

His hand hovers over one with a chocolate flower on top of it, but I can understand his hesitation. It's never wise to eat just anything in our fridge, as who knows what recipe (read: spell) my grandmother and mother are concocting next. Then again, since no spells will work on me, I figure I'm safe and scoop the small cake out from underneath his hand. I bite into it.

"Mmm," I say, licking icing from the corner of my mouth. "It's so good. Even if it probably is poisonous. Go on, I dare you."

Gabriel narrows his eyes at me, then takes the remainder of the cake from my fingers and eats it in one gulp.

"Some of it," my mother answers, inspecting a fork. "And stop hanging on that door," she admonishes absently. "It'll break again and I'm tired of having Chester fix the refrigerator. The last time he fixed it, it sang 'I'm a Little Teapot' every time I opened it. It drove me insane."

Gabriel inhales on a laugh, then begins choking on cake crumbs. Alarmed, my mother whirls around. "Which one did you eat?' she cries.

"The chocolate flower one," I say. "Will he live?" I help myself to another cake, this one covered in sugar violets. "Is this one okay?" I ask, and then pop it into my mouth.

My mother closes her eyes briefly. "Yes."

"Yes I'll live or yes the second cake that she just ate is okay? It's kind of important that you be specific here," Gabriel says.

"Yes to *both* questions." She opens her eyes again and glares at us before adding in a more casual voice, "Some catalogues came for you, Tamsin. And a letter from California."

Suddenly, the cake is too dry in my mouth, and I struggle to swallow it down. Gabriel raises an eyebrow at me.

"A thick letter or a thin letter?" I say at last.

"A letter letter," my mother answers distractedly. "Why?"

"Because I applied early admission to Stanford and it could be an acceptance or a rejection," I say, and brush my hand, sticky with crumbs, down the side of my jeans.

My mother turns, holding three forks aloft. "Stanford? What is this about?"

"It's a college in California," Gabriel says helpfully, then takes a step back as my mother glares at him.

"I know *what* it is. But *why*? I thought you were set on going to NYU. I thought you were staying in New York. Why would you be going all the way to *California*?"

I sigh. Most mothers would be pleased if their child got into Stanford. Not mine. She'd like nothing better than to have me live right here in this house in Hedgerow for the rest of my life, like generations of Greenes before me.

"I was in California once," a voice says, and then Uncle Morris blinks into view. My mother shrieks and drops all three forks on the floor.

"They have the loveliest wineries out there," Uncle

Morris says to Gabriel, who is trying not to laugh. Stroking his chin, Uncle Morris glances out the window. "I took a tour of this little vineyard once and had the most delightful Cabernet. The grapes were sweeter than honey that year, and—"

"Be quiet, Morris," my mother snaps, and then turns back to me. "Why would you leave New York? It's bad enough that you live in New York City for most of the year. I'm still not used to that, but why would you leave? And why would you let her?" she demands of Gabriel.

"Whoa," Gabriel says, putting his hands up.

"He doesn't control my—"

"That's not what I meant," my mother interjects. "Just why would you even need to go to college now that you've . . . now that everyone . . ."

"Now that everyone's decided to stop lying about me having a Talent?" I say blandly.

A silence descends over the room.

Uncle Morris clears his throat. "Ah, not everyone lied to you, Tamsin. I believe it was just your mother and father and your grandmother who even knew you had a Talent."

"And Rowena," I add cheerfully. "Don't forget about her. She'd be upset if you did."

"Thank you, Morris," my mother says bitterly, slamming the forks back onto the counter. "Thank you, as always, for being so helpful."

Uncle Morris blinks and his gaze shifts mournfully

toward the door. He starts to go hazy around the edges, but then Gabriel slaps him on the shoulder. "Hey, Uncle Morris, let's go play poker. I feel like winning some money."

Uncle Morris brightens. "All right. And I have a bottle I've been saving for just such an occasion."

"What occasion?" I mutter, but no one answers.

Gabriel kisses my cheek. "Later," he says against my ear, and leads Uncle Morris from the room.

My mother sorts silverware in silence for a few seconds. "I didn't mean that," she says stiffly after a moment.

I'm not sure what she's referring to, but I nod. "Okay."

"I just thought you would be happy . . . living here in Hedgerow with us . . . after school finishes."

"Come on, Mom. It's not like I'm the first person to go to college in this family." Then I pause. "Am I?"

"No. Of course not. It's just that I thought you would want to—" She blinks rapidly and presses the back of one hand to her eyes.

Wow. Planning this wedding must really be getting to her. I jerk open the refrigerator again and stare at the rows of cakes. "I don't *know* what I want, Mom. Half the time I forget that I even have a Talent and I think I'm just . . . ordinary, and then the rest of the time I walk around school remembering I have this big secret. I just . . . need to decide . . ."

"Decide what?" a deep voice says from the doorway.

My mother and I both turn to find my grandmother leaning against the wall. Her skin gleams almost translucent under the kitchen light, and the bones in her face seem to stand out sharper than ever. She's been ill for several months now and no one seems to be able to do anything about it.

"Mother," my mother says immediately. "You should be resting. Let me—"

My grandmother holds up one hand and my mother falls silent. Her dark eyes find mine and then some expression flickers across her face. Sadness? Unease? I can't tell. "Decide what, Tamsin?" she asks again, her voice clear and strong as ever despite her appearance.

Decide who I really am.

But I can't say that out loud, so I gaze at my grandmother helplessly. Her Talent is to read minds even though she apparently hasn't tried this on me for years, ever since she learned what my Talent was. But somehow she knows exactly what I'm not saying because she closes one eye in her trademark wink and says softly, "Ah."

"DOES THAT LOOK LIKE THE dress I put on hold?" Rowena asks the room out loud as I step across the threshold, holding the rose-colored dress that Agatha had pronounced so perfect for Rowena's wedding. "When I asked you to show me the dress that you're wearing for my wedding, I meant the dress that I picked out, the one on hold for you at Eidon. The one I instructed you to get. This one is rose colored. Rose. The one I picked out was silver."

"Gray," I mutter.

Rowena's eyes narrow and she steps off the pedestal that she's been standing on. Kicking her voluminous skirts aside, she marches toward me. "What?"

I squirm a little and flap one sleeve through the air. "Can't I just wear this one? I mean, no one is going to be looking at me anyway," I say, striving to appeal to her vanity.

"No, you cannot just wear this one," she says, her lip curling up as she glances at the wilted dress in my arms. "Where did you even get that *thing?*"

I probably shouldn't mention that I got it at a thrift store. Rowena loathes thrift stores, and she's already regarding the dress as if it's infested with fleas. "And what happened to the dress I sent you to get?"

"I didn't buy it," I say in a small voice, even though that should be completely obvious to her by now.

"What do you mean you *didn't buy it?*" Rowena asks, holding her arms out. Aunt Linnie makes a clucking noise, maybe because of all the pins she has clamped between her lips, and exchanges a look with my white-faced mother, who hovers in the background.

I shift from one foot to the other. "Um . . ."

"I asked you to do one simple thing for me, Tamsin. *One simple thing,* and you couldn't do it, could you?" My sister's voice is rising. "This is my wedding. My wedding. My special day. And you had to mess it up for me. Because you're Tamsin Greene and you think you're above all the rules now."

"That's not what I think," I say, stung.

"Rowena," my mother protests. The veil in her hands twitches sharply. "That's—"

"Don't you defend her, Mother. Not this time."

I blink. When has our mother ever defended me to Rowena? "I . . . it looked really awful on me," I finish lamely, and then try to backtrack, because one look at my sister's reddening face tells me this wasn't the best defense. "And it wasn't my size—"

"So what?" she hisses. "We could have fixed it. Aunt Linnie could have fixed it. I am the bride. I am the bride here."

"No kidding," I say, which only seems to inflame her more.

"Well, you're going back to the city to get it—"

"Fine by me," I say just as our mother says, "No."

The word falls like an ax through the rest of Rowena's sentence. The silence is broken only by Aunt Linnie's humming as she adjusts the last pin in the waistline of the dress.

"Your grandmother said that no one is to leave the property again."

"What?" Rowena and I both say at once.

My mother shrugs. "She doesn't want anyone leaving for the next few days."

"Why?" I ask.

My mother massages her right temple as if trying to drive away a sudden pain. The lines between her eyebrows deepen into what seems lately like their permanent dent. "She wouldn't say. Something she saw."

Errant sparks fly from Aunt Linnie's hands, and she exclaims softly, stepping back.

"Oh, for the elements' sake," Rowena says, swishing

her skirts out of the way and examining them thoroughly. Aunt Linnie wrings her offending hands in distress, but the ivory expanse of silk seems undamaged. My sister glares at me, then tromps to the door of her room and bellows down the hallway, "Silda. Silda, come here." Whirling back, she hisses, "You will match with the other bridesmaids. *You will if it's the last thing I do!*"

My mother and I exchange glances. "Uh, Ro," I say doubtfully, "I think you're taking this a little—"

"What is it?" Silda, our cousin, asks a little breathlessly as she enters the room. Tucking her wispy pale hair behind her ears, she glances first at me, then at my mother, and last at Aunt Linnie, who is still shooting sparks from her hands. "What's the problem?" she asks again, now in the tone that everyone seems to be adopting with Rowena lately. The "I'm not going to make any sudden moves or eye contact" tone.

I'm suddenly thankful for the three final exams that kept me at boarding school until today.

"That," Rowena says, pointing at me and my offensive rose dress. "That is what Tamsin thinks she is wearing in three days. To my wedding," she emphasizes in case we're not sure of the occasion that she's referring to. "Even though everyone else's dress is silver—"

"Concrete gray," I mutter, and as Rowena turns to glare at me, a smile slides across Silda's face so fast that I'm not sure it was ever there to begin with.

"Since Tamsin is being so stubborn and since Mother wouldn't dare send her back to the city to get the dress—"

"That's—"

"I need a favor from you," Rowena continues, disregarding our mother's protests. "I need you to change the dress to silver. Change it to match the others."

A prickly silence fills the room. Silda can change the surface appearance of an object. Shoes into stones, pebbles into diamonds. I don't know if she can manage a whole dress, but I sigh. If she can, then maybe we can avert this whole disaster that was, I admit, of my own making.

Shrugging, I step forward and spread the skirts of my dress.

It stays the exact same shade of rose.

"Tamsin," Rowena shrieks, and I jump. "Stop it. I know what you're doing and you're to stop it right now."

"What? What am I doing? I'm not doing anything," I say. "Sorry, Silda—is it too much? Can you—"

"Just let her change the dress," Rowena snaps, bustling forward, her cheeks turning the color of a brick. I stare at her for a second before realizing what she's saying.

"I'm not—"

"She's not stopping me," Silda says softly, and I turn to look at my cousin. If anything, her face is even more flushed than Rowena's, but she meets my eyes steadily. "I haven't tried to change the dress because I don't want her to try to stop me."

We all stare at Silda for a second until I am the first to recover. "Of course," I say bitterly. "You think I'm going to try and take your Talent." It's true that if someone tries to use his or her Talent against me three times, then I absorb it, but still, I would never do that to my own family member. Then I swallow sharply. I did do that to two of my own family members. One was Aunt Beatrice in 1939 and the second was an ancestor of mine who could throw fire in 1899. Still, it's not like I took their Talents *away* from them in the process.

And now Silda drops her gaze to the floor, but her voice is fierce as she says, "It's not right, Tamsin. It's not right that you can do that."

"I won't," I say. "I don't want your stupid Talent," I add coldly. "What good would it do me anyway?"

"Tamsin Greene," my mother says reprovingly as Silda lifts her head to stare at me. I match her glare for glare. My cousin and I used to be friends, or at least *friendly*.

"That's uncalled for," Silda says, frost coating her voice.

"Funny. I could say the same thing to you," I snap. "Sorry, Ro," I say, still staring at Silda. "Looks like I'm wearing pink after all."

"What? *This is my wedding*," Rowena shrieks, and we both jump. Then she takes a deep, slow breath and says to Silda in a voice that is soaked in honey syrup, "You will change her dress right now. You will change it to match the others and you will be delighted to do it."

Silda blinks slowly and turns to me, her hand outstretched.

"Rowena," my mother exclaims.

"That's right," Rowena says to Silda, ignoring our mother. "You want to—"

"Oh, stop it," I say irritably, and reaching out with my mind I pull hard in the way that I've learned. Suddenly the air in the room feels like winter as Silda blinks again and then steps back, her face pale. Her eyes dart to Rowena.

"You tried to compel me," she accuses my sister. Turning to me, she whispers, "And you stopped her."

"Don't bother thanking me," I mutter as I brush past her and out the door.

Darkness pours through the hallway of Grand Central Station, a darkness alleviated only by the occasional flash of lightning and by the four-faced clock, which is glowing with a cold white fire. Before my eyes, the clock begins to ripple and swell to five times its normal size.

Stop! I try to wake myself out of this moment, but I can't. I have to watch it play out.

One of the clock faces has now become a door that's swinging open. And all the while the hands are still spinning, spinning backwards, unraveling the moments and years.

Ten feet from the door, three figures seem locked in a strange kind of dance, arms and legs distorted by the clock's bright glare. Alistair is pulling my sister toward the door and the complete blackness that waits beyond it, while Gabriel has latched on to her other arm. Rowena twists between them like a rag doll.

"Rowena!" I scream. Alistair's eyes meet mine, chips of ice. "She'll never be free. None of you will ever be free," he hisses, his words carrying over the wind and the rain.

I jerk awake, my hands flailing outward as Rowena's twisted face shimmers and then fades into the pre-dawn shadows of my bedroom. Only then do I let myself blink and fall back against my pillows. I stare up at my ceiling for a while before turning my head to look out the window. The fields and forest beyond are hushed with the last breath of night, that perfect stillness just before daybreak.

She'll never be free. None of you will ever be free.

That last part's new, I conclude after a second. Usually the dream stops with Rowena stepping through the doorway. But this time Alistair's words have taken on a deeper twist. *None of you will ever be free.*

I grind my knuckles into my eyes, trying to rub away the last image of Rowena burning into a skeleton. This makes the third dream in a month. If this keeps up I'm considering asking my mother for one of those sleeping potions that she regularly doles out to Hedgerow's needy residents.

I pull the sheet up to my chin and flip my pillow. If I had these dreams only at home, I could use it as the perfect excuse not to come home, but the last one before tonight happened at school. One minute, Alistair was wrenching my sister's arm backwards as he pulled her through the open clock, and she was withering away into smoke. Then in the next minute, Agatha, with a head full of curlers, was standing over me, swinging the mop (that we never use otherwise) through the air over our heads. Later, after we had stopped giggling, she told me that she had woken up to me screaming and thought that someone had broken into our dorm room. I don't know if she was planning on scrubbing him to death or what. Poor Agatha. I can't be the easiest roommate in the world.

I sigh and look through the window again. Frost glitters across the fields. In three days it will be the Winter Solstice; Rowena's wedding day.

She'll never be free. None of you will ever be free.

"Mrrr," comes a small complaint from the corner of the room.

I flail upright again and then Hector, my grandmother's cat, leaps onto the bed. "Stupid cat," I mutter. My heart is beating as fast as it was when I first woke up.

"It's just a dream," I say out loud to myself, petting Hector's head a little too vigorously until he slaps at my hand with one paw. Luckily, he leaves his claws sheathed. "Just a dream," I say again.

Hector yawns once, then regards me through half-closed yellow eyes.

"Yeah, I know. I'm not buying it either." With my two index fingers, I rub small circles in my forehead, before standing up. "Milk," I announce. "Hot milk will make me fall asleep. Or at least that's what I've heard." And maybe Gabriel's still awake and I can persuade him to sit up with me.

At that thought, I smile and search out my pair of fuzzy bunny slippers that Agatha gave me as an early Christmas present. With their bulbous pink noses and goggly eyes, they're ridiculous, but I need some kind of ridiculous right now.

I crack open my door and stick my head out. The whole house seems to be silent and still and—

"Mrrr."

I jump again. Apparently, Hector understands the word *milk* because he's crept off the bed and is now winding around my ankles until I almost trip. "All right, all right, I'll feed you, even though it's the middle of the freaking night," I whisper, all too aware that I'm talking to a cat.

The stairs creak in their usual spots as I head down them. After one backward glance, Hector dashes ahead of me into the kitchen. I'm about to follow him when I stop, my head turned. A light is on in the small side parlor, and a murmur of voices, too low for me to distinguish, tugs at my ear. The last I saw of Gabriel he was locked in what looked like an all-night poker game with a red-eyed, grim-faced Jerom, who was insisting that he be allowed to wager his cuff links. Uncle Morris had apparently gambled away everything he had and then had conveniently fallen asleep over his cards. Why anyone continues to play cards with Gabriel is beyond me. I won't even play with him even though I have the Talent to stop him from "finding" all the aces every single time.

But now I inch closer. It doesn't sound like Gabriel or Jerom.

"No, I don't remember that," a voice says querulously, and I recognize it as Aunt Beatrice's. "Are you sure that happened, Morris? When did we say that? Now, back in 1939 I remember seeing a girl who looked a lot like her, but I think she was—"

"Are you sure it was 1939?" Uncle Morris breaks in.

"Of course, I am," Aunt Beatrice answers immediately. "I never forget a date!" Which is so patently untrue that I wait for Uncle Morris to laugh.

But he doesn't.

Instead he says, "Of course you don't. Here, have some more sherry, dear, and tell me—"

I tiptoe closer and peer through the half-open door to take in the scene before me. The parlor is lit by one slender red-fringed lamp and a dying fire in the hearth. The sliding doors that lead into the side garden are standing open, and cold air swirls into the room, raising goose bumps on my skin.

Uncle Morris, wearing his usual rumpled suit, is sitting very close to Aunt Beatrice on the love seat. As I watch, he rolls to his feet and deftly hooks two fingers around the neck of an opened bottle of sherry. He refills Aunt Beatrice's glass, but before handing it back to her he turns away and pulls something from his suit pocket. A tiny bottle that he swiftly unstoppers and tips backwards into his own mouth. Aunt Beatrice huffs with impatience.

Frowning, I focus in on my uncle's face. The way he moves, almost with a lazy, catlike grace, is so unlike his usual puttering motion that I can only wonder if the change has something to do with whatever it was that he just drank. As I stare at the scene before me, all at once Alistair's voice comes hissing back into my head.

None of you will ever be free.

"Here you are," Uncle Morris purrs, leaning over my great aunt.

Flinging the door open all the way, I scream, "Aunt Beatrice, stop. Don't drink it!"

Both Uncle Morris and Aunt Beatrice jerk their heads up. The glass slips between their open fingers and falls to the floor, the liquid spraying out in a shining arc.

"Tamsin," Aunt Beatrice snaps, her mouth working as

if she's not sure what to yell at me for first. But I can only stare at Uncle Morris as he leaps to his feet and grins at me, a wide *un*-Uncle-Morris-like grin.

"*Tamsin,*" he echoes, drawing out my name. "The name suits you so much better than—"

Reaching out with my mind, I slam up against the force that is *not* Uncle Morris and yank hard. All at once, a shimmering, twisting light pours from Uncle Morris's chest and reforms itself into a tall man with a mass of lion-colored hair. He is wearing dark formal clothes from another time, and as I stare at him, my mouth slightly open, he takes off his hat and tips it to me. "A pleasure to see you again," he murmurs. "But I do wish you had waited for the proper time. Your charming aunt was just telling me so many fascinating things about you all."

"Oh," Aunt Beatrice murmurs, crumpling off the couch to land on the floor. She clutches the collar of her green silk robe to her throat with knotted fingers.

"Stay back, Aunt Beatrice," I warn her and then stare at poor Uncle Morris's body. "What have you done to him?" I hiss.

The man glances down at my uncle, smiles again. "Him? He'll live. He might have even enjoyed the experience." And with that he nudges my uncle's body with one foot. Uncle Morris coughs faintly, but his eyes remain closed.

"Well, you won't enjoy this," I snap. Holding up one palm, I shoot a gust of fire directly at him.

At least I try to. Nothing happens. Not even a spark flutters out from under my skin.

The man lifts one eyebrow at me. "Impressive," he murmurs. "Truly. And now, having confirmed what I needed to, I'll be on my way."

Stunned, I hold up my other hand and try again. I imagine a pure jet of flame knocking squarely into the man's chest. But nothing happens.

"Aunt Beatrice," I scream. "Freeze him." I bolt forward as my aunt, who is now kneeling beside Uncle Morris, raises her head, gives me a doubtful glance, and then tries to stand. But her feet are tangled up in her bathrobe sash and she tips sideways, giving a little whimper as she goes down.

The man clicks his tongue against his cheek and shakes his head in a mock sorrowful fashion. "And this is the legendary Greene family? How in the world did you people ever triumph over us?" he asks, spreading his hands to the ceiling as if seeking the answer there.

Not wasting any time with words, I shove my hand toward his forehead, intending to freeze him. But he side-steps me easily, knocks my hand aside, and then captures both of them between his own. He pulls me up against him and we stare at each other, our faces inches apart. And even at this very inopportune moment, I notice that he has the most unusual eyes I have ever seen, pale gray with definite streaks of silver that wheel outward from his pupils.

Stop staring into his eyes, you idiot!

But still, I can't look away, and he seems to understand that, judging by the way his full lips curve into a delighted smile. "It was *such* a pleasure," he murmurs as if we're alone in the room. "I do wish we could have gotten to know each other better." Then he pauses, seems to consider. "Well, perhaps I do have a moment. And who could resist you?" And before I can even react, he leans down and kisses me fully on the mouth.

I struggle, but then suddenly the whole world narrows down to the feel of his mouth on mine. The hazy thought that I've never kissed someone with a mustache before enters my head before a wave of cold clarity breaks over my skin. The usual reaction when someone is trying to use a Talent on me.

The next second he's released me and I stumble backwards. He smoothes the corners of his mustache, then says lightly, "Another time?" as if asking for a rain check.

"Oh, and please, don't be angry with your young man. He did put up a very good fight, after all. I'd hate to be the cause of a lovers' quarrel."

I stare at him blankly for one second. *Gabriel? What happened to him?* Furious, I swing my hand at him again, but he steps sideways.

And vanishes in midair.

The wind whips through the still-open French doors, swirling through my hair.

"Oh, dear," Aunt Beatrice whimpers. "I don't think he was who I thought he was."

I sink to the floor, next to Uncle Morris's body. "No kidding," I mutter, dragging the back of my hand against my lips.

THREE

"HE SAID IT WAS SUCH a pleasure to see you?" my mother exclaims for what must be the third time. She raises her mug of tea to her lips but puts it down again, untasted as far as I can tell. "Why? Why would he say that?"

I still don't have an answer for her, so I stare at my own cup of rapidly cooling tea. Better than looking around the room, confronting the fear and worry on everyone's faces. My mother and father, awakened by Aunt Beatrice's yelps, rushed down the stairs two minutes after the stranger had disappeared. Disheveled with sleep, they listened to my stumbling and confused account of what had just happened, made even more stumbling and confusing due to Aunt Beatrice's querulous interjections and the sight of Uncle Morris moaning on the floor. At which point my grandmother had walked slowly into the parlor, leaning heavily on Rowena, and I had to start the whole story again.

My grandmother had listened silently until my voice stuttered to a halt. Then she sent my sister to the stillroom, and when Rowena returned clutching a small brown bottle, she had tipped most of its contents down Uncle Morris's throat. The room suddenly filled with the scent of honeysuckle and black pepper and glue, and Uncle Morris had coughed and gagged and screwed his face up until I was fervently glad that I wasn't the one drinking that stuff. But whatever it was seemed to work, because he sat up and demanded in a rusty-sounding voice that I bring him a real drink, right away. My mother had tried to question him as to what happened, but he shuddered, swilled half his glass of wine in one swallow, and repeated that he couldn't remember anything after falling asleep on the couch earlier in the evening. Beatrice finished her own glass of wine, then eyed Uncle Morris's half-full glass hopefully, and that's when my mother had told them both to get some rest. After that we had all made our way into the library, where my grandmother had sunk slowly into her favorite chair, seemingly lost in thought.

"Why would he want to meet Tamsin?" my sister asks suddenly from where she's sitting next to our grandmother.

"Thanks," I say, but my heart isn't in it because she looks so tiny in the green armchair. Plus her face is too pale and she's methodically rubbing her left wrist against the side of her bathrobe.

She flashes me a look that I could interpret in my sleep, then sits up straighter and addresses my grandmother. "We need to consult the book. We need to get a glimpse of the future so we know what to do, what to think about"—here she lifts one hand, gestures toward the window as if to encompass the outside world—"all of this."

As if compelled, all our eyes swivel to the book lying closed on the library desk. The heavy black cover is embossed with twining leaves and arcane symbols that blur in my vision as I think back to the last time I was in this library with my grandmother. The words that she uttered then come swirling back into my head:

I can see nothing for our future. Nothing, as in, we will no longer exist. The pages are empty in a way that they never have been before.

Now I stare at my grandmother, willing her to speak. She brings one hand to her forehead, her fingers pressing and kneading the wrinkles there. "It's no use," she says at last, and I look down as everyone turns back to her.

"But why?" Rowena protests after a moment, and I have to wonder at how bleak everyone must be feeling, since normally my grandmother's word would never be questioned. "We've always consulted the future to under-stand the—"

My grandmother drops her hand and says, "Look to the past this time, Rowena—1887."

My sister seems about to object, but then stands up

and approaches the book. "Wouldn't you rather . . ." Her voice trails away. I study my tea again.

"I don't have the strength anymore," my grandmother says at last, her voice as deep and steady as ever.

Jerking my head up, I look at my mother and then at my sister. They both look grave but unsurprised.

My mother stands up abruptly, knocking over the cup that she has balanced precariously on the edge of her chair. Dark tea soaks into the rug, but she doesn't seem to notice as she joins my father at the window, her arms swinging a little with displaced energy. Both of my parents lean forward as if bracing themselves against a bitter wind.

Rowena murmurs a single word and then opens the book. I stare down at my hands, flexing my fingers cautiously. I try to shoot a small spurt of flame at the tea-stained carpet by my feet, but just as before, nothing happens. My skin doesn't even tingle the way it used to before the fire erupted from my palm.

Looking up, I catch my grandmother's eyes on mine and I immediately clasp my hands together in my lap again. I had left out that small detail of no longer being able to use the power of fire in my general account of the evening. The sound of whispering pages pulls at my attention, and I stare at my sister. Her lips move soundlessly, one finger skimming down the length of the book as she reads. Then abruptly, her face goes even whiter than before.

"What is it?" my father says, stepping forward. His hands clench by his side. Reflexively, I check the sky outside the library window, expecting a violent storm to blot out the wisps of sunrise-pink clouds at any second.

"This wasn't here before," my sister whispers. She throws a quick look at my grandmother, who gives a tiny nod, then continues, *"In 1887, in the dying days of October, just before Samhain, a stranger arrived in New York City, claiming to know more than he possibly could. He was seen calling upon La Spider, the matriarch of the Knight family."* Rowena lifts her head again to stare blindly across the room, while crumpling the long fingers of her hand into a fist. "Alistair. He made it back there."

"We have to do something," I snap. "We're not going to just sit here and let him try, right? He's gone back to a time before . . . before the Domani exists. He's going to tell the Knights about it. What if our family can't make the Domani because of what he tells them? What if the Knights . . . win?"

My family was forced to create the Domani in 1887, when the Knights, a rival witch family, began to threaten the Greenes and their way of life. Somehow they managed to capture all of the Knights' power, isolate it in one object—the Domani—and assign a Keeper for it. Over the generations, the Keepers changed. For safety's sake, no one knew who the Keeper was at any time. And no one knew what the Domani was, since it kept changing its appearance, too. Outside of the Keeper no one was able to touch the Domani and still live.

Except for me.

Back when I'd thought Alistair Knight was really Alistair Callum, just a professor at NYU, I'd agreed to help him find a lost family heirloom. I hadn't known then who the Knights were, what the Domani was, or that I actually did have a Talent. I hadn't known a lot of things. But I did find the Domani. Once as a wall clock in 1899, once as a pocket watch in 1939, and once in the present day as the clock in Grand Central Station. And then I became the Keeper. For now.

"But what if he doesn't succeed?" my mother asks the room in general. "If he's Traveled back to 1887, how long can he last there anyway?"

"What do you mean?" I ask, because no one else seems confused by that statement. Everyone gives me blank looks until Rowena, adopting her favorite "Clearly I know more than you know and that's the way it will be until the end of time" tone, answers me.

"It's a rule of Traveling. A Traveler can't stay long in the place that he's Traveled to before he suffers ill effects."

Tightening my fingers on the handle of my mug, I ask, "Ill effects?"

"Death," she says succinctly.

"Oh." I sit back in my chair and contemplate this. Just a few months ago, Gabriel and I had Traveled twice, but we never seemed to suffer any ill effects. Then again, we were in 1899 and 1939 for less than an hour each time. "How long?"

"Well, no one really experiments with this, Tam," my sister says, frowning at me. She seems on the verge of adding something else, but then doesn't. I can tell that she's still wondering how I managed to Travel back to 1899 and 1939. Only my grandmother knows that Gabriel took me and not the other way around.

"Three days," my grandmother says suddenly. "I remember that from our history. Three days is generally the limit."

My mother seizes on that. "Maybe he won't be able to do much in just three days?" she asks hopefully.

Rowena and I both resume staring at my mother. "Are you kidding me?" I ask. For once, my sister doesn't even bother with words. Yanking back the sleeve of her robe, Rowena thrusts her arm forward. Faint scars glimmer on her skin.

A slow rumble of thunder sounds in the distance. My father's jaw is set.

"Obviously, he's succeeding," I whisper. "Otherwise, why was this stranger able to come here tonight?"

"Camilla," my grandmother says, her voice quiet and

even. "Everyone. Leave the room. Everyone leave, except Tamsin."

Two spots of color blaze suddenly in my mother's cheeks, but she turns and leaves the room without another word—although she does throw a pretty eloquent burning glance at me. My father follows, and last of all my sister, who closes the door softly behind her.

The fire cracks through the otherwise silent room, and I get up, cross to my grandmother's chair, and kneel by her side. She puts her hand on my hair, smoothing back the curls from my forehead.

"I have to go back," I say finally. "To 1887."

She sighs. "I know."

Shadows skip across the hearth, pooling around the paws of the china dog statues that stand at attention on either side of the fireplace. I hold up my hands again as if asking my grandmother to inspect them. "I lost it. I tried to throw fire at the stranger tonight and couldn't. Why?"

My grandmother shifts in her chair. "I wondered about that. I suspect your powers of assimilation are only temporary. As in, you can borrow other people's Talents, but only for so long."

"How long?" I ask slowly, turning my hands over, examining the tips of my fingers.

"That I don't know. See if you still have Beatrice's power."

I quit examining my hands to look up at my grandmother. "Now? On you?"

"Well, unless you see anyone else in the room," my grandmother murmurs.

"What if I can't . . . unfreeze you?"

My grandmother snorts. "It does wear off. After a week. And I highly doubt you're going to lose it between one blink of an eye and the next."

I swallow as my grandmother juts her forehead toward my trembling fingers. Her sweetly sharp scent wraps around me as I reach up, touch her brow with the lightest of taps. She stills into immobility, her eyelids frozen in the act of blinking. In a sudden rush of panic, I tap her forehead again, harder than the first time, and she draws in a breath, leans back. "Well, that answers that. You still have the power to freeze people."

"For how long?"

"You acquired it a week or two after you acquired the power of fire, yes?" I nod. "So you have a little time perhaps."

I swallow, then voice my most pressing fear. "I have to go alone."

My grandmother leans back and closes her eyes, and I try not to notice how the skin sags around her jaws, leaving the bones of her cheeks to stand out in sharp contrast. "I suspect Gabriel will have a hard time with that," she says at last.

"I know, but how can I let him come with me?"

My grandmother opens her eyes and regards me down the length of her nose. "I don't know that you can *let* him do anything, Tamsin."

I duck my head and try not to think of how incredibly angry Gabriel's going to be with me if I don't at least give him the option. But I can't. Not after what Rowena told me tonight about the long-term effects of Traveling.

"Those effects of Traveling—that doesn't apply to me, right? I mean, nothing else seems to touch me so—"

"I doubt that Traveling will harm you in the same way that it does other people. Nothing seems to apply to you in the normal fashion," my grandmother adds wryly. "Remember, it's up to you to allow when a person's Talent can work on you and when it can't. It's entirely your choice."

This I already know, since I was able to let Gabriel take me back to different times. But now I voice my next niggling thought. "Still, if I ditch Gabriel, it's going to be impossible to Travel back anyway. We only Traveled twice, so I don't have that power." Visions of tricking Gabriel into using his Talent on me three times while I secretly resist scurry through my head, leaving me with a bitter taste in my mouth. But there seems to be no other way.

"Of course, there is another way," my grandmother says now, and I look up with a start, then remind myself that she can't use her own Talent of walking through my mind unless I let her.

"How?" I ask.

She regards me for a moment as if expecting me to come up with the answer. And then I do.

The Domani!

FOUR

I'M HALFWAY BACK TO MY room when a shadow crosses my path. "Tamsin," Gabriel says, and then has the foresight to clap his hand over my mouth, muffling my scream against his palm. I glare up at him and then bite his thumb for good measure.

"Ouch," he says, shaking his fingers.

"You shouldn't have scared me like that," I hiss, expecting at any moment my mother to come charging down the hallway and order us all back to bed, where if she had her way we'd have pleasant dreams as well.

"Sorry." Gabriel shrugs. "I was awake and I saw the lights go on in the library and then I saw your parents at the window, so I came over to see what was happening."

I nod. Gabriel must have been staying at his mom's apartment. Ever since Aunt Lydia returned from California, she's been living in the apartment over the barn.

"What's happening? Why are you awake?"

"Bad dreams, and then they came true."

"What? Tam, you're not making any sense," Gabriel adds as I remain silent. He shifts to lean against the wall.

"Listen, it's late and . . ."

Gabriel folds his arms and gives me an overly patient look.

"Okay," I sigh. "It seems we had a visitor. Who has the Talent to jump into other people's bodies."

Gabriel takes a second to digest this. "How'd you find this out?"

"I—" I cast another look down the hallway toward my parents' room. A light suddenly snaps on underneath the doorway. "My room," I whisper.

"He was in your room?" Gabriel says, loud enough to wake up the whole stupid house.

"No," I hiss. "Let's go to my room now."

"Tamsin, I thought you'd never ask—" Gabriel says in an entirely different tone.

"Oh, shut up." Wrapping my hand around his elbow, I tug him down the hallway and into my room, then close the door with a soft *click*. I listen for a second but hear nothing before turning back to Gabriel, who is now staring at my feet.

"What are you—oh." Blushing, I kick off my pink bunny slippers toward the bed.

"Tell me about this visitor," Gabriel says.

"I woke up from a . . ." I swallow.

"The usual?" Gabriel asks, and I nod. He reaches one hand out and with his long fingers, kneads the back of my neck.

"So, I went downstairs and I saw Aunt Beatrice and Uncle Morris in the parlor." Closing my eyes briefly, I add, "Only it wasn't Uncle Morris." Quickly, I fill Gabriel in on the rest of the evening, including what I didn't tell the rest of my family, that I can no longer throw fire.

"Why would he say that? 'Your young man put up a good fight.' You've never met him." We're sitting side by side on my bed now.

Gabriel shakes his head. "I don't know. But if I do see him again I'll be putting up more than a good fight." He drums his fingers against my knee until I put my hand on his. Probably should have omitted the part about the kiss. We hold hands in silence for a few seconds until Gabriel says, "So, it seems like we're headed back to 1887. If we want to stop this before it starts."

I swallow, then tug my hand away gently. "About that. I think you—"

"Don't even think about it," Gabriel advises, his eyes intent on mine.

"What? All I'm saying is that you should—"

"Not happening."

I roll my eyes to the ceiling before looking back at him.

"Would you just let me fin—"

"No," Gabriel says. "You're not doing anything alone. You hear me?"

"I—"

"Do you hear me?" he repeats, his voice completely calm and even.

But just then my bedroom door is flung open. "What is going on here?" my mother says, bursting into the room. She is flourishing a candlestick through the air.

Even though absolutely nothing is going on, Gabriel and I both dive to the opposite ends of my bed, our gazes pinned to my mother, who is turning the exact same shade as my bunny slippers.

"Tamsin Greene," my mother begins, slowly lowering her arm. "I specifically told you to go to bed." Then she turns on Gabriel. "And you, Gabriel Snowe. Out. Now." She cracks the words through the air like a whip.

Gabriel gives me one burning glance and says, regardless of my mother, "It's not like you can go anywhere without me anyway."

"Good point," I say. Not true, but I'm not going to mention that now.

Apparently, my mother doesn't like what she's hearing. "No one is going anywhere tonight except to bed. *Now.*"

He bolts off the bed and ducks past my mother, one arm over his head as if to ward off a blow from her candlestick.

My mother draws in a deep breath, her eyes scanning the room as if searching for anyone else I may be hiding in the closet before looking back at me. "Bed," she says, apparently determined to speak in one-word directives. With her arms folded, she waits until I actually climb under the covers.

"Good night, Mom," I say meekly. She snorts, flicks off the light, and closes my door.

I blink through the minutes until the darkness has faded from the corners of my room. Then I tiptoe to my door and listen. I wouldn't put it past my mother to be waiting outside. Easing the doorknob to the left, I pull the door open and glance down the hallway in both directions. Nothing but the usual shadows. Reminding myself that I have very little time left, I slip out of my room for the second time that night.

Good thing my family never seems to throw anything out. I spent the past half-hour stumbling around the dark attic, rummaging through box after box. Now I stare down at the items I've finally chosen. One long black skirt, two semi-tattered lace-covered petticoats, one black long-sleeve button-up vest bodice thing with a hole under the right arm and grayish stains on the cuffs, and two black shoes, the kind with hooks and laces. The heels are worn, but otherwise they seem in good shape. I slip them on, wiggle my toes, and begin the process of doing up the laces. They're slightly too big, but I'll live. I hope.

Next, I pick up the skirt and shake it out. Dust motes glitter and swirl in the early-morning light of my bedroom. Sneezing, I lace myself into the petticoats and then the skirt, spider web lace brushing across my bare legs. Then I stuff myself into the bodice, doing up the horn buttons while dealing with another sneezing fit in the process.

Finally, I confront myself in my bedroom mirror. I look like I just escaped from a mental asylum that doubles as a nineteenth-century thrift shop. Sighing, I pin up my hair in what I hope is a respectable-looking knot. Then I can't put it off any longer.

I slide open my top dresser drawer and sift through my extra socks and underwear until my fingers just brush against a thin chain. My stomach flips once, then settles, and I curl my thumb and forefinger around the metal and pull the object into the light. My clocket, as I used to so fondly refer to it. The locket flashes its silver face at me as it swings in the air like a pendulum. Eventually it stills and I regard the closed lid with trepidation.

Maybe because I've slept all of three hours, the soft click of my door opening is not enough warning. "I knew it!" my sister hisses.

Startled, I drop the locket. At least she has the consideration to shut the door before advancing on me. Then she stops and takes in my outfit. Her lip wrinkles up in what seems like the start of her trademark sneer, but the effect is immediately ruined by her fit of coughing as she inhales a cloud of dust. "Where did you get that outfit, anyway? The Sneezation Army?"

I give her a look. She knows I particularly love shopping at the Salvation Army. "The attic," I mutter.

"You can't seriously be thinking what I think you're thinking?"

"Oh, you think?" I respond politely, but she ignores me.

"You're not going back."

"I don't know what you're talking about," I say. I crouch down, my new/old skirt bunching around my legs, and pick up the locket between careful fingertips. I set it back on my dresser, all too aware of my sister's scrutiny.

"What did you and Grandmother talk about after I left?" Rowena asks while winding the sash of her cream-colored robe around her fingers. I study my sister for a few seconds in silence. With her pale hair and skin, you'd think she'd be totally washed out in a cream-colored robe, but no, as usual, she looks dazzling. Her complexion has taken on an extra smoothness and luster; her eyes are burning.

I shrug. "Nothing important."

"Oh, really? Then you won't mind telling me, since it's nothing important," Rowena persists. "You know Mom's going to ask you just as soon as she gets up again, and—"

"Mom doesn't want to know anything, Ro. She doesn't want to face what's happening."

"And what exactly is happening?"

I shake my head. "Nothing. It's late. I'm tired. You're tired. Shouldn't you be getting your beauty sleep? You know, the big day and all."

But now my sister's eyes flare wide open, an angry-cat green. "Don't think for one second that just because you've discovered that you have Talents that you can treat me like . . ."

I stare at her. "Like what?"

"Fine," she snaps. "I'll find out on my own."

"What—" I start, and then stop as she whirls out of my room. I follow her to the doorway, watch as she charges down the stairs. "Where are you going?" I hiss after her. The soft *thunk* of the library door closing is my only answer.

I lean against the doorjamb, frowning. Earlier, I had helped my grandmother back to her room before my excursion into the attic, so unless Rowena is preparing to consult the book again for a record of our conversation . . .

I dash out of my room and down the stairs. At the foot of the steps, I stumble in my too-big shoes and crumple onto the landing, amid another cloud of dust from my skirt. Stifling a sneeze, I pick myself up and hurry toward the library, half expecting the door to be locked. However, the knob turns easily in my hand and I start forward, my eyes on the book, which is resting in its usual place on the blotter. But the book is closed. My eyes dart to my sister, standing with her back to me in front of the fireplace as if contemplating the dying flames.

Then she lifts her hand in a graceful gesture and I freeze as a yelping voice reaches my ears. Words are pouring out of the china dog statue's mouth—my words. *"Still, if I ditch Gabriel, it's going to be impossible to Travel back anyway. We only Traveled twice, so I don't have that power."*

I stare at the dog statue standing to the right of the fireplace. Its jaws are open now, trembling slightly, even though its glass eyes are as flat as ever.

"What—" I hiss, and step forward, but then the dog statue on the left answers in a deeper growl of a voice. *"Of course, there is another way."*

"How?" the first dog asks again, and then gives a mournful bark.

I reach out with my mind and the dogs fall abruptly silent, their jaws freezing back into place, their voices stilled in their china throats again.

Rowena turns slowly and faces me, drawing the lapels of her robe closer to her throat. "How indeed?" she says softly. "I *knew* you weren't able to Travel on your own," she adds.

"Yeah, congratulations. That's really important in the grand scheme of things."

She looks at me thoughtfully. "It is, isn't it? I mean, if you *ditch Gabriel* as you said earlier, how will you get back to 1887?"

"I didn't say that's . . . " Then I pause as something clicks into place. "Who else can Travel in this family?"

"What?"

"Who else? Who else has *or had* that power?"

Rowena shrugs. "Apparently, no one's had it for generations and generations."

"And what about in the Knight family? Did anyone have it there?"

"Well, obviously that man, that stranger tonight did, or—"

But I've stopped listening to her because the growing suspicion in my mind is too overwhelming. What if he didn't have that Talent? Or rather, what if he didn't come by it naturally? What if—

"Tamsin," my sister snaps, and I start out of my reverie. She steps forward, her face looking suddenly tired in the pale morning light. "Tamsin, you may not realize this, but I want to help you. I want to come with you."

"No," I say immediately, my mouth dry. "Don't you remember what happened to you the last time you met Alistair?"

My sister's lips tighten briefly. Rowena had spent seven miserable days under a love spell, if you could call it that. A spell that Alistair had made with her own blood, which forced her to do his bidding. My family had watched her grow weaker and weaker, powerless to stop her from running back to Alistair every chance she could. Only when

Alistair had vanished through the doorway of the clock in Grand Central Station had the spell been broken. "What if you come back with me, and we see him, and the spell reactivates or something?"

"It doesn't work like that," she says exasperatedly.

"Sorry," I say blandly. "Considering I've spent most of my life thinking I had no Talent at all, I'm doing my best to catch up here."

Anyone else would have the decency to act faintly embarrassed, especially if they played a part in keeping that information from someone. Not my sister, though. Instead, she presses on with "Which is exactly why you need me to come with you. You'll need help, Tam. You can't do this alone."

"I can—"

"Nobody could do this alone."

"I—"

"What's your plan, then?" she challenges me. "Are you going to knock on La Spider's door and set the house on fire? Oh, wait, I forgot, you lost that Talent already, haven't you?"

I glare at the china dogs, wishing I had smashed them into smithereens before they revealed that part. "I have a plan," I say.

My sister raises one eyebrow, and then when I don't answer, says, "Well? Enlighten me."

I shrug. "I need to go back and warn our family that

the Knights are going to attempt to control them through blood spells. And that Alistair is going to help make that happen and make it impossible to stop the Knights unless our family acts sooner than our history says they did. And I'll tell them that the Domani they're supposed to make isn't going to work forever, so they need to remake it. Better. They need to make it stronger . . ." I add, my words trickling off lamely.

My sister raises her other eyebrow now. "Brilliant," she says succinctly.

Somehow I get the feeling she's being sarcastic.

"All right, well—"

"That's brilliant. Warn our family. Especially in 1887, when Traveling is forbidden and they're really likely to believe you. And then you're going to tell them that something they haven't done yet, and haven't even *thought* about doing yet, is not going to work anyway in the future so they need to *do it better*. That'll really go over well."

"Doesn't anyone read the book in their time? Won't they be able to read the future and understand what happens?"

Rowena stares at me. "Wow. You really know next to nothing about how the book works, don't you? You don't just flip open the book and read the future like you're reading a recipe. Besides Talent it takes strength to even . . . wrestle a few of the words onto the page. They're . . . slippery at best. If you're lucky you get to see phrases, glimpses of what *may* come to pass. It's not all laid out there like a newspaper article."

"Thankfully, we have you," I mutter. "I suppose you're amazing at it."

My sister regards me coolly. "I'm not, actually. But I'm the best besides our grandmother, who's most likely the best this family's ever seen. And even she couldn't prevent all this from happening. So, that should tell you how hard it is to understand the book. And how do you plan on finding them, anyway? Our family in the nineteenth century?"

I shake my head at her. "What do you mean? The house on Washington Square Park—"

"Was bought by our family in 1895."

"Oh," I say.

"It's not like you can just head back there and look them up in the phone book, okay? They didn't have phone books then, you know."

"Gee, thanks for the tip." I cross the room, rubbing my arms against the cold air that's seeping through the cracked window. "You know, I think I can manage this. I mean I did find the Domani, after all."

"Yeah, and look how well that worked out," Rowena mutters. Then she shakes her head, "Besides, you had significant help. Gabriel." She circles the room once, then again, the hem of her robe swirling around her calves. Other people's robes would just flap, but no, not Rowena's. "So just how are you planning on getting back without him?

You can't . . ." Then she nods her head once as if confirming something. "The Domani. You're going to use it."

I swallow. Only my grandmother and Rowena know that I'm the current Keeper.

"I'll only be gone for a couple of days. Long enough to find our family and warn them, then I'll come back. Just in time for your wedding." I try to smile, but my sister stares at me.

"Even if you manage to get there using the Domani, you do understand that it won't work again to get you back. You'll have gone back to a time when there is no Domani, so how are you going to get back?"

Somehow I know my blithe answer of *I'll figure something out* isn't going to work on Rowena. My other answer of *I'm probably not going to make it back* isn't something I even want to think about. "Give me three days, Ro. I'll find them, I'll warn them, and then I'll find a way to get back. Just tell Mom I went back to the city to pick up the dress. That I felt so guilty—"

Here my sister snorts, something that would seem inelegant when done by anyone else. "She'll never believe it."

I shake her grip off. "*Make* her believe it," I say.

My sister turns pale. "I can't use my Talent on Mom."

"And Gabriel," I add.

"I can't use it on either of them. You—"

"You used it on Silda," I say.

"That was different. That was about a dress. This is

just a *little* more serious." She holds her thumb and forefinger a millimeter apart.

"Please, Ro. I need a time to try and do this on my own. I don't need anyone else getting hurt. You heard what the stranger said tonight. *Don't be angry with your young man. He did put up a good fight.* Don't you get what that means?"

My sister starts to shake her head, and then her eyes widen. "He Traveled here. Using Gabriel's Talent. Which means Gabriel Travels to the past and—"

"And they get him. Somehow. But that doesn't have to happen. That can all be changed."

But my sister gives my wrists a little shake. "Three days. You're coming home. No matter what happens. Three days, Tam, and then you'll find a way home, no matter what. Promise."

"I promise," I whisper. "In time for your wedding."

I've never felt so bad lying to my sister.

"There," Rowena says, pinning the last of my curls into place and turning me by the shoulder to face the mirror. "You look somewhat respectable."

I blink. Rowena has managed to tame my hair into a tight knot and has pinned and tucked me into my costume, mending the worst of the rips and tatters. She also made me remove the two silver studs I had in my right ear and the two pink hearts in my left. "And, here, take these," she adds, metal glinting between her fingers.

I look down at the small hoard of dollar coins, fifty-cent pieces, and copper nickels she pressed into my hand. I can't help but smile. Uncle Chester had given us each a few of these old coins throughout the years, and we used to fight over them all the time. "I knew you stole these from me."

"I did not," Rowena says. "You lost yours. These were from *my* collection. Anyway, I made sure none of them was from after 1886, so you should be safe."

I slide the coins into the inner petticoat pocket, where they feel agreeably heavy. "I promise not to spend all of these at once," I say, because the weight of everything else I should say is pressing at my throat. And then, because there's nothing left to do, I pick up the Domani very carefully by the chain. With a deep breath, I release the catch. The locket springs open and I brush my finger against the glass face.

Between one ticking second and the next, the clock hands freeze in place. Tiny letters begin arranging themselves into an inscription on the back of the open lid. Letters written in a language that I'll never be able to understand. "Hurry, Rowena," I whisper.

For one horrible instant I think my sister has changed her mind when she folds her lower lip between her teeth. Then she leans forward and reads the inscription in a soft, trembling voice: "Fire in the East and Water for the South, Air for the North and Earth in the West. All of these now Blood does bind. Yet even now Time erases what Blood would buy."

We stare at each other.

I find my voice first. "That's not what it said—"

"The last time," she says, finishing my thought.

A cold wind curls around my ankles, pulling at my clothes, and a splinter of lightning stabs across the blue sky outside my bedroom window. All at once, dark clouds race from the west to meet the growing light in the east. Glancing down at the watch in my hand, I notice the tiny second hand is spinning wildly backwards, followed more slowly by the hour hand. I reach out, brush the air above my sister's shoulder, careful not to touch her. "Tell Gabriel . . . tell him I love him. That I'm sorry," I whisper.

Rowena frowns. "Tell him yourself, Tamsin. When you see him in *three* days." Then she narrows her eyes at me. "You're not—"

But whatever else she is going to say is lost as my windows rattle violently under the sudden onslaught of the storm. The Domani is burning in my hand, but I tighten my fingers anyway, and then the ground buckles once violently and darkness presses down across my eyelids with a weight that I can't endure. I black out.

FIVE

WHEN I OPEN MY EYES it's to find that I'm sprawled under a tree, bands of sunlight criss-crossing my faded black skirt. The sky overhead is a bright aching blue, and golden-red leaves drift like snow through the air. I pull myself to a sitting position, blink, and take in two small, solemn-faced children, a boy and a girl, standing just a few feet away from me. The boy sticks his thumb in his mouth, his eyes wide and round, while the girl holds a large wooden hoop in front of them both like a shield.

"Hello," I say, my voice cracking a little.

They both jump, and the boy jams his thumb even farther into his mouth and starts sucking it furiously. Finally, the girl speaks. "How did you do that?" she asks, her voice wavering.

"Do what?" I ask as I dig a pine cone out from under my knee. I don't trust my legs yet. My head's still spinning and there's a weird empty sensation in my chest as if my heart is trying to drop down into my toes. I take a deep breath. I made it. I think.

"You appeared out of the air."

"Oh, that." I wave one hand and the little boy ducks behind his sister. "Listen, never mind about that. Can you tell me the date, first of all?"

The girl's mouth curves downward and her pale eyebrows scrunch together. "How can you not know?"

"I just . . . don't."

"October twenty-eighth," the boy said. "Nanny is going to give us candy apples on Beggars' Night."

"Beggars' Night . . . oh, Samhain," I say. Three days before Samhain. Alistair must have just arrived. *A stranger appeared in the dying days of the year.* There's still time to stop him. There has to be.

The boy takes a half step out from behind his sister's skirts, and after pulling his thumb out of his mouth he says, "Are you one of them? The ones who walk on Beggars' Night?" He is eyeing me hopefully. "Can you do magic?"

But now his sister turns her frown on him. "Don't be foolish, Collin. We wouldn't see her in the daylight if she were." Then she turns back to me. "That's what Nanny calls it," she adds suddenly. "Samhain. But Mother doesn't like—"

"Collin. Eugenia," a female voice sputters, and then a second later, a middle-aged heavy-set woman, dressed in black with a white cap bobbing loose on her head, trundles toward us. "Where did you children get to?"

"She fell asleep," Collin whispers to me. "She always falls asleep in the park."

I glance at the woman's sun-scorched face while finally attempting to climb to my feet.

"What mischief are you at?" the woman huffs as she hurries over to them. A sloshing liquid sound accompanies her movements. Abruptly, she claps one hand over her skirt pocket. The sloshing sound stops.

"We were talking to the lady. She just appeared under the tree. Like one of your spirits that you—"

"Hush now," the woman says, glaring at me as if I'm the one who claimed to be one of her spirits. She brushes down Collin's pants with what seems like a little too much force and then produces a smaller and more delicate white cap from her skirt pocket. "I found this on the bench, missy," she says to Eugenia, who scowls again but lets the woman settle it on her head.

"I told Collin she's not one of your spirits," Eugenia says, her voice thickly smug. As the woman jerks the laces into place under her pointed chin, Eugenia reaches out and gives her brother a pinch on his arm. "I told him that since we could see her—"

"Hush," the woman says again, and gives me another sidelong glance, her gaze sweeping me from head to toe. "I close my eyes for a second and the two of you run off. Talking to strangers and all. You'll both be the death of me, that's what," she mutters, giving Eugenia's laces one final tug.

Just then a black and red carriage glides past us, the driver holding the reins tightly, staring straight ahead. The passengers, three girls around my age dressed in brilliant blues and scarlets, are giggling riotously as their glances skip over me. Even though I know it's silly, I sigh, trying not to look down at my black skirt.

The woman straightens up, watches the carriage pass, and then takes both children by the hand and begins to lead them away.

"Wait," I call after their retreating backs. The woman halts and turns, but just barely. "I'm looking for a family. The Greenes. Do you know them or where they live?"

"Never heard of them," she says, and, lifting her nose in the air, she marches off. Collin gives me one forlorn glance over his shoulder, and I heartily wish I had taken the time to freeze his horrible nanny just for a minute so he could at least be satisfied. Even if that would have been an incredibly stupid idea, it still would have been fun.

I take a deep breath and turn in a slow circle to get my bearings. I'm standing in what appears to be a park, with pathways curving left and right. Somewhere to my right, a fountain is gurgling and the shrieks of more children ring out across the grass. Trees, blazing with autumn golds and reds, surround me, and here and there through the branches I glimpse rows and rows of brick houses that look oddly familiar. It takes me a second and then I pinpoint it. Washington Square Park. I probably landed here because I had been thinking of my family's townhouse, which is—or I guess will be—on the north side of the park. I stare through the trees again, noting that there are definitely more of them than I'm used to. Turning northward, I search for where the huge stone archway should be. Just a few months ago, Agatha and I had taken turns snapping each other's picture under it when we took a prospective NYU student tour.

There's no archway.

And now the ground seems to tip and spin beneath my feet, and for one second I feel a stab of fear. Maybe I'm not immune to the symptoms of Traveling after all. I put one hand out and press my palm against the rough bark of a tree to steady myself. *Relax. You knew everything was going to be so different. And it's not like you haven't done this before.* Then I swallow, trying not to remember that the last two times I Traveled, I had Gabriel with me and a guaranteed way of getting home. But thinking about Gabriel is not an option, otherwise I really will start crying. I stare down at my other hand, which is still clutching the Domani. I hold the little locket up to my ear. Just as I thought, the clock is no longer ticking. The way home is truly going to be a mystery. I slip the locket over my neck, close the catch firmly, and, steeling myself, I step onto the nearest path, searching for a way out of the park.

SIX

I FEEL LIKE ONE OF THOSE tourists that Agatha and I always used to sidestep around back in my own New York City. The ones that walk too slowly and stop right in the middle of the sidewalk so that you almost trip over them. The ones that fling out their arms, pointing and staring and exclaiming. Okay, well, at least I'm not pointing and staring and exclaiming, but I'm pretty sure my jaw's dropped a couple of times.

This New York is so different from my New York. For starters, I can see the sky. There are no skyscrapers, no clusters of buildings reaching for the clouds. These buildings are all a lot shorter. And there are no cars and no people on skates and no joggers. Instead there's a parade of carriages drawn by horses jolting over cracked cobblestone streets.

Which means mud.

A lot of mud. The hem and lower half of my once black skirt is now flecked brown, and I can't say it's adding much to my look.

"Oysters, oysters, oysters! Get them fresh," a man shouts as he pulls a cart past me, the wheels coming dangerously close to my toes. Right after him comes a stout woman screaming, "Hot pies, hot pies! Get 'em while they're hot!" A large basket is slung over her right arm.

My stomach rumbles loudly and I step forward, waving my hand timidly. Instantly, she swerves across the path of an oncoming carriage, causing the driver to curse and haul on the reins. "How many?"

"One," I venture.

"Meat or fruit?"

"Ah . . . fruit?" Probably safer.

With a nod, she plucks a pie out of the basket. Twisting it up in brown paper, she says, "That's a nickel, love."

I fumble through my change, noticing her eyes skip downward at the clink of coins in my skirt pocket. Finally, I pull out one of the nickels Rowena gave me and place it in her square, chapped palm. She hands me the pie and the heat of it fills my hand.

"Please," I say as she's about to plunge off into the traffic again. "I'm looking for some people. The Greene family. Have you heard of them?"

But she's already shaking her head. "Sorry, dearie." Her eyes skim over me once again. "New to town?"

I nod.

"Looking for work?"

"Um . . ."

"Where's your family? Runaway, then?"

"Sort of," I offer at last, since it's what she's going to think anyway.

She's already nodding. "Don't you go down to Five Points. You stay away from that crowd. You don't need to go looking for work there yet. Things aren't that bad, I hope. Too many girls end up there," she sighs, and then abruptly she wheels off into the crowd again. I break off a corner of the crust and nibble it, then suddenly begin shoving large pieces of the pie in my mouth, not caring if I burn my tongue.

After wandering down Broadway for another hour and almost getting killed twice, once by a speeding two-seat carriage and once by what looked like a bus pulled by six horses, I find the nerve to pull open the door to what looks like a bar, called the Lion's Head. But once I'm inside, it's all I can do not to run out again.

The room is dim, as if the sunlight gave up trying to fight its way through the streaked and grimy windows. Smoke wreathes the low, uneven ceiling, and the floor is scattered with sawdust. Although the level of noise remains the same, all at once I can feel eyes on me. Mostly men crowd the bar and fill the tables, but here and there a few women loll on stools or drape themselves over the men's arms. Someone shrieks with laughter and I jump, my feet already turned halfway to the door. Then

I straighten up, biting the inside of my cheek. *Nothing's going to get done, Tamsin, if you don't try.*

Channeling Rowena at her best, I walk toward the bar in what I hope looks like a calm, cool, and collected manner. I place my hands on the sticky wooden counter, widen my elbows slightly to avoid having anyone bump into me, and stare at the bartender until he slowly moves my way. Since he takes so long, I have time to notice that he's huge; his shoulders and arms look like they're carved out of rock slabs. "What'll it be?" His voice is a growl and he stares at the air over my shoulder, so I abruptly stop channeling Rowena and go for Agatha.

I give him a perky smile and say, "I'm looking for a family called the Greenes. They live around here. Have you heard of them?"

His gaze finally shifts to mine and then he gives one shake of his massive head. "No. Can't say I have."

Of course he hasn't. I sigh and review my options on finding my family. Town crier? Taking out an ad in the paper? And what paper would that even be? I bite down hard on my tongue, trying to think.

With one meaty paw, the bartender unhooks a polished glass from the rack overhead and fills it behind the bar before placing it in front of me with a surprisingly gentle motion. "Drink that. On the house," he adds as I stare up at him.

Before I can thank him, he moves away, responding to the call of another customer down at the end of the bar.

I take a cautious sip of my drink. Not bad. As I wipe foam from my upper lip, a small man in a bowler hat settles on the stool next to me. He is dressed in a gray suit with a curl of lace at each cuff that flutters as he waves one arm at the bartender. But the bartender resolutely ignores him, and so the man turns to me and gives a despondent sigh. "New here, are you?" he says at last, eyeing my beer wistfully.

Am I wearing a sign on my forehead?

"Um . . . sort of, yes."

He nods excitedly. "I can always tell. Always tell." His nose twitches as if sniffing out information, and suddenly he reminds me of a ferret. "And what brings you to the big city?"

I take another sip of my beer while considering the wisdom of talking to strange men in bars. In another century. "I'm looking for a family."

His eyes sharpen and then linger on my chest. Suddenly, the beer leaves an unpleasant film on my tongue.

I'm about to find another seat when he says, "I know lots of people in this city. What's the name?"

Turning back, I watch as two more men and a woman in a low-cut blouse and a skirt settle in noisily on his other side. One of the men knocks an elbow carelessly into the small man's arm, and he flinches but otherwise doesn't protest. "The Greenes," I say at last, noting that this man's eyes are never still. They rove constantly across the bar top, my glass of beer, my folded hands, and beyond to the door. He frowns, cocks his head a little, then shakes it. "No," he says finally. "Never heard of them. The Greenes. That's a common enough name. Your family?"

Almost automatically, I shake my head. "No. Friends of my mother's from long ago. I thought they might be able to find me work." Shrugging, I swallow my disappointment with more beer.

I study my glass, considering my options, when he says casually, "So you are looking for work, then? I could find you a nice position, since you're new to the city." He blinks his eyes rapidly.

Before I can help myself, I reply, "Oh, sure—and next you'll tell me that you can sell me a piece of the Brooklyn Bridge."

Has the Brooklyn Bridge even been built yet?

But the man only grins at me, revealing stained teeth. "You've got spunk. I like that." He leans in closer. "A lot of girls who just come to the city meet a bad end. But I can help you. If you need work, I know of a family that's hiring."

"Hiring for what?" I ask, suspicion still bright in my mind. I edge away a little. The man smells like vinegar.

"Domestic help." Then he taps the brim of his hat, regards me with wounded innocence. "Whaddya take me for?"

I'm spared from answering because the bartender lumbers back over, still ignoring the little man, who straightens up on his stool like a child suddenly at attention.

He pulls three foaming glasses of beer for the people who just came in, then casts me a measured sidelong glance. I nod at him and he nods back, and suddenly, I decide that he might be my new favorite person in this century.

"I'd like a pint, Joe," the little man quavers. The bartender swings his head down and stares at him, unblinking.

"Show me your money first."

The man lets out a sigh but rummages through his pockets and finally extracts two dull nickels from somewhere inside his waistcoat. He puts them on the bar slowly, his fingers edging them across the scarred wood. The bartender slaps his meaty paw down on them and they vanish. "That was for last week," he says, winks at me, and lurches off.

The man crumples on his seat. "Anyway, this job won't last long."

"That's nice," I say absently, trying to formulate a plan. Finish my beer, start going from door to door and asking about the Greenes? Where would they have moved *from* in 1895? Then a horrible thought occurs to me. What if they live out of the city? Somewhere in the country? In three days I'm not going to be able to cover much ground.

Gradually, I become aware that the man's voice is still buzzing in my ears. "Solid family. Very wealthy. Lots of girls looking for work these days would kill for this position."

"I'm sure they would," I murmur. If Gabriel were here now he could just find my family for me. Pressing my fingers into the bar counter, I try to blot out that thought just as the man leans in and taps his nose. "My niece," he says confidingly. "She works there now. She was just telling me that they needed a new girl."

I stare at him for a moment, and then ask idly, "What happened to the old girl?"

The man shrugs. "Run off. With the lady of the house's jewelry, no less."

Turning my glass in circles, I consider my options again. Taking out an ad in a newspaper seems like the best idea. Although in three days how anyone in my family is going to see it and contact me is something that I don't feel like worrying about right now. "So why don't they advertise in the paper?" I ask, studying the ring of moisture left on the wood. "And speaking of which, what paper is the best to advertise in? If I were trying to—"

He draws back a little as if I took a swipe at him. "Oh, sure, and have every bit off riffraff knocking on their door." I give him a sideways glance, noting that the lace at his right cuff is stained yellow and tattered-looking. Now that I look at him closer, his clothes look in worse shape than mine.

"Oh, well, sure, keep out the riffraff and all. That's where you come in. Right." I straighten up. "Well, this has been pleasant and all, but . . ." I pick up my glass to drain the last of my beer.

The man shrugs. "Suit yourself, then. I just thought a nice girl like you who's new to town and doesn't have any family might want a nice job. But turn up your nose if you want to. Not every girl would be so foolish as to say no to working for the Knight family."

The glass slips from my hand, tumbles to the floor, and shatters. But the sound is lost in the general press and crush of bar noise. The man's eyes shine a little in the gloom. "Ah, heard of the family, have you?"

I shrug with studied casualness. "Who hasn't? I read the papers."

He nods rapidly. "Of course. They're always invited to all the balls, the dinners—they're top of the line. I could put in a good word for you with my niece. She could rec-ommend you."

"And what do you get?" I ask boldly. "Other than the joy of helping a poor *penniless* girl new to the city?"

He clasps his hand to his heart, reviving his air of wounded innocence. "Only that you think kindly of old Horace Merton should I ever need a favor or something."

"Horace Merton?"

He tips his hat at me. "And your name?"

"Agatha," I say rapidly, and then I want to kick myself. Alistair knows Agatha's name.

But it's too late to take the name back, so I search around for the most innocuous last name I can. "Smithsdale," I add.

He thrusts out one damp-looking hand. After a second, I offer him mine. His grip is weak and I pull my hand away easily. But he doesn't seem to notice. Instead, in a cheerful voice, he says, "And now if you'd like, we could call on my niece. You know, to recommend you to the lady of the house."

Inwardly, I shiver at the idea of meeting La Spider. Still, if I can't exactly find my family yet, I can do the next best thing. I can keep an eye on their enemy. My enemy. Maybe I can even stop Alistair from ever coming to the house.

I nod, then stand. "Take me to them."

Horace hops off his stool and claps his hands. I turn, my eyes roving across the bar until I find the bartender, who's watching me impassively. He narrows his eyes at Horace and shakes his head. I give a little shrug and a smile, trying to convey that I know what I'm getting myself into. But the bartender doesn't seem convinced.

Come to think of it, neither am I.

SEVEN

"AND THIS IS THE NEW Delmonicos," Horace says, gesturing expansively toward a five-story building made entirely of white marble as we walk up Madison Avenue. Craning my neck I can see that it takes up all of Twenty-sixth Street. For one instant, I try to remember what exists there in my time, but I can't. Agatha and I don't usually hang out around Madison Square Park.

"Delmonicos now has three locations, but this is the grandest. They have a ballroom on the second floor, all done up in red and gold. And silver chandeliers on the first floor and a fountain surrounded by flowers. Lady Knight dines there all the time."

I cock an eyebrow at Horace. "Have you ever been inside?"

He touches his hat as if to adjust the fit. "Sadly, no. I just heard all about it."

I nod and we continue walking. Horace seems to have appointed himself as my personal tour guide and has taken to the role with zeal, which includes grabbing my elbow at opportune moments to steer me around puddles and pulling me out the way of passing vehicles. "It's coaching season," he explains now as we leap out of the way of a gleaming black carriage that zips past us. "All the gents and ladies dress up in their finest and up and down they go." As he chatters he pulls me around another yellow-tinged puddle and then quickens his pace. As we turn down Twenty-seventh Street, he recites the numbers. "Fourteen, sixteen, eighteen, and here we are. Number twenty. The house of the Knights." His voice drops dramatically and I wonder if he's going to take off his hat and kneel right then and there on the cobblestones. I try not to let my expression slip from the wide-eyed country girl I'm supposed to be.

The Knights' house is wedged in a row of similar-looking brownstones, but somehow it seems to stand out. Maybe it's the elegant flourish of the wrought-ironwork stair rails or the sleepy gaze of the two stone lions guarding the entrance.

Maybe it's that the lead case windows suddenly seem like too many eyes watching the street below.

I shiver and Horace turns to me solicitously. "All right, then? We'll just call on my niece now, mention you're looking for a job." I start toward the front door in a daze. "This way. The servants' entrance," he hisses. Recovering, I follow him through a small black gate set off to one side of the brownstone. Horace digs through his pockets, that vinegar smell of his rising sharply as he searches, until finally he produces a thin wrought-iron key. With a flourish, he unlocks the gate and beckons me after him.

The back of my neck feels damp, and I have the sudden vision of the two stone lions springing up from their crouch to pad silently behind us. Unable to stop myself, I look over my shoulder. Only the gate and a glimpse of the street beyond. We walk down the winding path, Horace bobbing a little ways in front of me, until we reach a large back garden. Immediately I notice that the garden is immaculate, almost as if it's frozen. Unlike my father's gardens and orchards, where plants seem to bloom in a vivid and glorious tangle, here not a single leaf dots the crisp grass and all the plants stand upright in soldier-straight rows, straining toward the unreachable sky. A large sundial is mounted on the wall, guarded by a lone statue of a woman. I study the statue more closely. It's not a classical Greek or Roman replica that I would expect to see in the Knights' backyard. Instead, the features are coarser, the face dominated by a thick nose and square chin. An expression of pain or surprise is stamped on the woman's face, and her head is bowed as if in remorse or misery. I take a step toward her, struck by the thought that if Rowena were here she could make this statue speak about everything she's seen. She'd probably have a lot to say.

"Hurry now," Horace hisses. He has taken off his hat

and is twisting the brim of it in his hands over and over until I want to point out that he's going to crush the thing. But I follow him down a small flight of stairs and wait next to him as he rings the copper bell that hangs in the center of a black wooden door. So close, Horace's vinegar smell is starting to overwhelm me, and I notice that small pearls of sweat are dampening his hairline. Suddenly, he looks at me. "You have done this kind of work before? Domestic service?" His eyes bore fiercely into mine.

Great time to be asking me that, I want to say, but I'm starting to feel a little sorry for him, especially with the way his hands are shaking, and so I nod. "Sure." I don't think the occasional dusting of my dorm room shelves and shoving things under my bed or Agatha's really counts, but I'm not about to mention that now.

The door swings open and a tall girl about my age wearing a black dress and a white apron blinks out at us suspiciously. Her blond hair is drawn tightly back against her head. Her eyes rove over me and then settle on Horace. If anything, her suspicious look deepens.

So much for family goodwill.

"Horace," she says flatly.

"Rosie, my dear," Horace cries in what seems to me a pretty good avuncular tone. He steps forward as if to kiss or hug her, but she leans to one side and so he settles for a clumsy pat on her shoulder. Immediately, she shrugs him off.

"What brings you? I didn't send for you," she says now, still blocking the entrance with her body. "I don't have any money to—"

"Well," Horace blusters grandly over the rest of her sentence. "This is Miss Agatha Smithsdale, a most delightful young woman who happens to be a little down on her luck right now. She's looking for work. New to the city, she is. And then I remembered that you mentioned the house needed a new maid—you know, since the last one did run off. So I brought her here to you." He beams at us both as if inviting us to share in his joy at his own brilliance. Then when the girl says nothing, but continues to regard us with her flat gaze, he asks, "The position hasn't been filled yet, has it?"

Rosie looks at me dubiously, her eyes examining me from head to toe. "It's for a lady's maid. You've done that kind of work before?"

I nod.

She leans against the doorway, folds her arms. "You can do all the hairstyles, then?" I nod. Does it count that once I cut off Rowena's hair in her sleep?

"Worked with a hot press?"

Deciding that *hot press* is a nineteenth-century term for an iron, I nod again. No one needs to know that I'm philosophically opposed to ironing.

"What's the best way to remove a stain from a ball gown?" she fires at me suddenly.

Okay, I'm sensing a dry cleaner is not an option here. I scrounge my brain for nineteenth-century stain removal techniques. "Baking soda and lemon water," I say with as much authority as I can. "It worked wonders at my last position."

The girl regards me coolly for a minute. "And where was that?"

"Chicago," I say, figuring it's far enough away.

"And you have references?"

Beside me Horace draws in a breath.

But I'm ready for that one. "Unfortunately, no. The woman I worked for was elderly. She died . . . suddenly," I say, letting my voice tremble just the slightest bit. "I didn't think to ever get a reference from her, and then her son inherited everything, and he . . . he was a cold man and . . . so, I came here. With all my savings."

Horace nods. "That's a terribly sad tale, Miss Smithsdale," he says softly, and then looks at Rosie. "She has no family."

"None at all," I echo.

Rosie exchanges a long look with Horace and something in her shoulders seems to ease. For the first time she smiles at me, revealing two charmingly crooked top teeth. "I only ask because the Lady will ask you all these things again, you know," she confides. "She's not here right now, so we can get you up to snuff on anything you need," she adds.

"Where is she?" I ask. I can't decide if I'm disappointed

or relieved that I won't have a chance get a glimpse of La Spider today.

"She and the young miss went upstate to Lord Roslind's Hudson estate for a wedding." Rosie says this very grandly. Horace looks impressed, so I try to as well. "They'll be back later today. She left the hiring to the Undertaker. And she'll be right angry that he hasn't found anyone yet. But now that you're here . . ." Here Rosie lowers her voice and sucks in her cheeks until they pucker.

"Who is the Undertaker?" I ask.

Rosie rolls her eyes and exchanges another look with Horace. "Mr. Tynsdell. The butler," she adds. "So, we better smarten you up and all or you'll never pass. You'll be lady's maid to Jessica, the young miss. And *she* doesn't notice anything. She's in her own world, that one." She steps back and beckons me in. "Is that all you have with you?"

I nod.

"Not even a change of clothes?" Her tone is politely incredulous, but I can see the doubt scrolling across her face.

"I . . . was robbed. On the train platform in Chicago," I say, lowering my eyes a little. It's best to keep it brief when lying.

Rosie gives a little sigh. "I'll see what Livie left."

"Who's Livie?"

"Lady's maid before you," she says, her voice suddenly lower.

"I thought she ran off. Didn't she take everything with her?" I ask now, glancing up just in time to catch another look passing between Horace and Rosie.

"That's right," Rosie says easily. "She did. But she may have left a few things here and there. Well, come in, then. Not you," she says to Horace now. She pushes him back out the door, muttering something to him while fussing with her apron. A small metallic *chink* reaches my ears and then I see Horace dip his hand quickly into his pocket. Apparently, Rosie found some money after all. Horace bobs his head once in my direction and then turns away. The door swings shut behind him.

My eyes strain to adjust to the sudden darkness of the hallway. "Follow me," Rosie says as she brushes past me, and I do, trying not to trip. We climb a cramped staircase to emerge into a bright and sunny kitchen lined with racks of gleaming pots and pans. A large black stove takes up one end of the room, buttressed by counters that have a well-scrubbed look. A small fire burns in the hearth at the other end. A thin gray-haired woman is sitting at one end of a long wooden table, cradling a cup of tea between two reddened hands. With wide eyes, she takes me in, and then looks questioningly at Rosie.

"New lady's maid," Rosie says with a shrug, and pushes me forward. "Cook, this is Agatha Smithsdale. Agatha, this is Cook."

Cook shuffles to her feet and presses my hand within

hers. Her eyes search mine swiftly, and then she looks down and says softly, "Pleased to meet you, dear." Something about her face, or maybe the way her hair curls in tight sprigs at her temple, suddenly looks familiar. But then the impression fades.

I open my mouth to say something similar back when the faint sound of a door closing penetrates the kitchen, followed by a jaunty whistling tune.

If anything Cook grows even paler, but it's Rosie's reaction that really fascinates me. Smoothing quick fingers over her hair, she refastens a stray wisp with a pin and then pinches her cheeks three times while biting her lips. "Be right back," she murmurs with a wink, and then dashes out of the kitchen.

"That's not Mr. Tynsdell, is that?" I venture. Maybe I could scrub my skirt in the sink before he meets me? Cook shakes her head, compresses her lips, and shuffles over to a cabinet. She removes another mug from the shelf and fills it with tea from a white pot on the counter. "Drink this, dear. While you can."

A little unsettled by that last comment, I accept the mug, staring down at the hot amber liquid, and give it what I hope is a very unobtrusive sniff. It smells like nothing more than strong black tea. Watching me, Cook gives a little grunt and something like a smile touches her lips. "You're not so dimwitted as the others that come through here."

"The others?" She sighs and sits down as if standing is suddenly too much to bear. "How many others?" I venture.

She shrugs. "They never last long."

"I heard the last one, Livie, ran off," I say casually, and sit down, too, blowing on my tea to cool it.

A sudden silence chills the room. Glancing up, I watch as the woman takes a sip of her own tea, her hand trembling just slightly. "That's not true," she says hoarsely, and suddenly puts her cup down with a clatter. "She died." Her fingers twitch toward her cup as she whispers, "Poor lamb, she got sicker and sicker, and they kept—"

But her mouth freezes around whatever else she was going to say as the kitchen door swings open and a giggling Rosie backs into the room followed by a tall man dressed in a rumpled white shirt and dark pants. With a wide sweeping motion, he tips his hat to Cook and then flips it up in the air, letting it tumble over and over before catching it and handing it to Rosie.

I set my cup down too fast and the hot liquid slops out over my fingers.

But he doesn't even look at me. "Cook," he says, his voice filling up the spaces of the kitchen effortlessly. "I'm famished. And you're just the lady I need to help me with that."

"I'm not surprised, Master Liam, seeing as you didn't come down to breakfast."

He winks at her. "Don't scold," he says, laughing. "You

know I can't bear it. And how could I come down to breakfast when I wasn't even home? Now what about one of your famous omelets? That should do it. Oh, and if you have any bacon and coffee."

"Very good, sir," Cook murmurs, and rises to her feet again. "I'll send it up to your rooms," she says.

But he gives her a wounded look. "What, and deny me the privilege of your company? You'll do no such thing. I'll eat it here." Then he lowers his voice to a mock whisper. "Just don't tell Mother when she returns. You know how she likes to stand on ceremony." With a loud sigh, he sprawls into a chair and pulls Rosie onto his lap.

Cook's face stiffens in a polite smiling mask and she bobs her head, then moves over to the giant stove.

Please don't notice me. But of course it's too late. As if hearing my very thoughts, the man turns the full force of his electric silver gaze on me and smiles. "Well, *hello,*" he murmurs in a very different tone than the one he just used with Cook. Rosie straightens up in his lap, her gaze darting back and forth between us.

I swallow and jerk downward in my best imitation of a curtsy. Then, with my heart slamming frantically against my ribs, I raise my eyes and look fully at the man who I last saw in the parlor of my family's house.

The man who kissed me and disappeared.

EIGHT

TO MY RELIEF, THE SILVER eyes don't flicker with any sign of recognition. "And who's this?" he says, turning his blond head down to Rosie.

He doesn't know me, he doesn't know me. Relief fizzes through me until my knees wobble and my fingertips tingle. Which means I've arrived before he Travels to my family's house. Which can only mean one thing. Alistair hasn't called on La Spider. Yet. All these thoughts churn through my head at warp speed.

"This is Miss Agatha Smithsdale," Rosie is saying now, and I tune back in, trying to smile and nod as if everything is completely normal and I'm not facing one of my family's mortal enemies. "She's come about the new position. Lady's maid to Miss Jessica."

"Ah yes," the man says, stroking the lines of his pale golden mustache. "Well, my mother should be back soon. Has she met our Undertaker yet?"

Rosie giggles. Cook slams a pan on the stove, breaking

eggs into it with what seems like unnecessary force, but neither Rosie nor Liam looks in her direction. "Not yet. But he should be back within the hour."

Liam winks at me. "Nothing to it. Just nod and smile and call him sir and let him pontificate and you should be fine."

Before I can answer, the doorbell rings. It sounds unnaturally loud in the kitchen. Rosie sighs, brushes her apron off, and squirms out of Liam's lap. "Whoever it is, I'm not at home," Liam says cheerfully, adding cream from a small silver pitcher to the steaming mug of coffee that Cook has set before him. "I'm going to eat and then go to bed, and I don't want to deal with any of Mother's endless callers."

Rosie ducks out of the kitchen again. Unsure whether to sit or not, I look at Cook for help, but all I get is a view of her back and the rigid lines of her shoulders as she slaps bacon into a pan. Then Liam makes it easy for me. With a wave of his cup, he motions me to sit.

"So, Miss Smithsdale," he begins. Just then the sun slides through the kitchen window, pouring across his throat and one side of his face. He stretches a little and rubs long fingers across his neck, and I swear if he were a cat he'd start purring. I'm not into the nineteenth-century look, but I'd have to say that Liam is pretty attractive. Remembering exactly who he is and what he did to my Uncle Morris helps me to squelch that thought.

Focusing those silver eyes on me once more, Liam asks, "Where are you from?"

"Chicago," I say, folding my hands neatly in my lap, my eyes downcast as the smell of bacon begins to perfume the air.

"Ah, Chicago, yes, I've been there. Brilliant city. Tell me, where did you live?"

I bite my lower lip, then offer what I hope is a shy smile. "Oh, sir, nowhere you would have visited, I wager. It wasn't a very grand neighborhood."

Wager? Grand? Maybe I'm laying it on a little thick.

But he gives a rich chuckle, revealing perfect white teeth. Apparently, he's lucky or has great genes, as I'm pretty sure that orthodontia doesn't exist in the 1880s.

Cook sets a blue china plate in front of him, spilling over with a huge omelet and several slices of bacon, and then deposits a thick white linen napkin and a shining fork and knife on the table. He tips an adoring gaze up at her, but she bustles back to the stove without a word. After shaking out the napkin, he tucks it around the edges of his lap before wielding the fork and knife with gusto. I look away and hope that my growling stomach can't be heard over the vigorous washing up that Cook is now absorbed in at the bathtub-size sink.

"You'd be surprised," he says finally after some thorough chewing. "I don't confine myself to merely *grand* neighborhoods. So—"

I'm saved from further questioning by Rosie's reentrance. An unreadable expression skims over her face when she sees me sitting at the table, but then she swivels her head to Liam as he asks, lazily, "So, who was it? Let me guess, Lady Hopewell with her two unbearably ugly daughters? Or perhaps Lady Rehnquist with her three even uglier daughters, if such a thing is possible?"

Rosie giggles as expected and then makes as if to swat his arm playfully. "No such thing. A Mr. Alistair Callum looking to speak with your mother. He said it was most urgent." Under the table, I press my feet together until I feel a blister on my left toe ping in protest. *Not so soon*, I want to howl.

Liam raises an eyebrow but returns to his omelet after a second. "One of those endless horrible charities, no doubt, always looking for a handout. Did you tell him no one was home?"

"Of course," Rosie says. Then she frowns. "I told him she wasn't home and he said he'd call again. But he seemed . . . upset. Odd, really."

He grunts, chews a piece of bacon. "Those charity types often are. Why they'd choose that as their life's calling, I couldn't begin to imagine." And he shudders before stuffing down the last piece of bacon.

Cook appears at his elbow to take the plate away. "It's a noble calling," she says to the air above his shoulder. "A charity worker. Helping unfortunate folk. We could all follow that example a little more. To make up for all our sins." Her quiet voice throbs through the air. Rosie and Liam both stare at her in silence.

Then Liam smiles that perfect smile again. "Don't you think of running off, Cook. You're needed here. *We're* your favorite charity."

"Charity is not what keeps me here," she says quietly, and then steps back as if afraid she's said too much.

But Liam only laughs and ignores her last statement. "As for me, I'll choose to help out poor orphan girls, like Miss Smithsdale here. That can be my charity," he murmurs, his eyes meeting mine intently.

I swallow and try to smile, but my stomach is roiling, although this time it's not from hunger. Alistair will come here again. Somehow I have to stop him. But before I can even figure out a way to do this, the kitchen door opens yet again and another man enters quietly. He is dressed in a stiff black suit and carries a newspaper folded in crisp pleats under one arm. His eyes roam across the entire kitchen as if gathering evidence before settling on the table and on Liam lounging there. His mouth tightens almost imperceptibly, and then it twists up into what must be his idea of a smile.

"Hello, Robert," Liam booms out, stretching his legs farther under the table.

"Master Liam," Robert replies quietly, and then, "Cook, Rosie." His voice narrows on the last two words, and Cook hurries forward and hands him a cup of tea, which he accepts with only a brusque nod. His eyes flick back to Rosie, then zoom in on Rosie's hands, which rest on Liam's chair. But her face is impassive and her hands remain where they are. His mouth does that twisty thing again. Then he turns to me, raising one dark gray slash of an eyebrow. I stumble to my feet, throwing an imploring glance at Rosie.

"Mr. Tynsdell," Rosie says, her voice carefully blank. "This is Miss Agatha Smithsdale. She's come about the new position."

"Very good," Mr. Tynsdell says quietly. "And how did you hear of it?"

I open my mouth, then look past Mr. Tynsdell's shoulder to where Rosie has widened her eyes. She shakes her head once, a quick fluttery motion. Then she looks directly at the newspaper tucked under Mr. Tynsdell's arm. I'm momentarily confused, because Horace said it wasn't in the paper, but then Horace seems kind of full of it. "I read it in the paper, sir," I say, and he nods once, appearing unsurprised.

"Of course Lady Knight will wish to interview you, but—"

"No need," Liam says lazily, locking his arms behind his head. "I already did. And I found her qualifications to be quite satisfactory."

I try not to snort. Apparently, having a pretty face is

about the only qualification needed if Liam's doing the hiring. Somehow, I get the idea that La Spider won't be so easily convinced.

Mr. Tynsdell's lips tighten again. I'm guessing that he does this a lot. "Be that as it may, Master Liam, I think that I should—"

Liam sits up, turns his leonine head slowly, and pins Mr. Tynsdell with his gaze. "I said she's qualified. Shouldn't that be enough?" All of a sudden his voice has gone soft. Over by the range, Cook's arm freezes in the act of reaching for a dishtowel and Rosie bites her lower lip as if to hide a sudden smile.

The air seems to shimmer and I blink and then blink again. *Liam* seems to be shimmering as Mr. Tynsdell's face shifts into the color of ash. "Very good, Master Liam," he says tonelessly, one hand fingering the collar at his throat as if it's choking him.

For a split second I think about stopping what Liam's doing. It would be so easy to just reach out with my mind and figuratively slap his Talent in the face. But if I do that I'll blow my cover before it's even been established.

Liam holds the butler's gaze for another second, then turns back abruptly and laughs, looking solid again. "After all, man, it's not like there's a hundred applicants knocking on the door." Then he winks at me. "Don't take that the wrong way." And with that, he shoves back his chair and clambers to his feet, stretching out his arms to the ceiling. "I could sleep for a week," he announces. With a cheerful wave, he exits the kitchen.

After his departure the air seems charred and too close, and I lock one foot around my other ankle.

"Sit and have your tea," Cook says softly to Mr. Tynsdell, who nods, then stumbles to the table. Cook sets a fresh teapot down in front of him along with a plate of bread and butter. "Eat up," she coaxes. Then she turns to Rosie and says, "Don't you have something better to do?"

Rosie draws herself up and gives Cook a scornful glance. "You'd best watch yourself," she says slowly, and then, looking at me, she makes a sharp *come here* motion with her hand. "I'll show you around," she says, and then adds pointedly to the air above Mr. Tynsdell's head, "since Liam says you're staying."

Mr. Tynsdell lowers his cup back to the table. "That's *Master* Liam to you," he says sharply.

But Rosie just laughs and flounces from the kitchen. After a second I follow. But not before I catch one last glance from Cook.

She looks afraid for me.

NINE

"AND THIS IS THE LAUNDRY room, although Lady Knight employs a laundress, so we just have to press their gowns and fold their garments," Rosie says while sweeping her arms around the white-walled room. Earlier, she had paraded me past a dizzying array of rooms, each one seemingly larger than the last, full of walnut-stained paneling and marble floors and so many paintings that I could hardly tell the colors of the walls. Frescoed ceilings depicting blue skies and frolicking cherubs, and thick velvet drapes and tables crammed with clocks and books and miniature stone statues all blur into one solid idea: clearly, money isn't an issue for the Knight family.

"And here's where we sleep," Rosie says, leading me down the hall. The contrast between the rooms below and the room we're standing in now is like a splash of cold water in the face. This room is small and triangular, with two narrow iron-framed beds, each spread with a nubby white quilt and a single pillow. A matchstick-legged table stands between the beds, and a dresser with a blue ceramic pitcher and matching wide-lipped basin just about complete the scene. With a sudden horrible thought I kneel and look under one of the beds. Then the other. Only empty white floorboards covered in a thin scrim of dust. Still on my knees, I look up at Rosie, who is frowning at me in bemusement.

"We . . . we don't have to empty their chamber pots or anything, right?"

She widens her eyes. "*Chamber pots?* No! They each have their own bathroom. In marble."

I nod but persist with "Um, and do we have a bathroom?" I ask. "I mean, we don't have chamber pots or anything like that?"

Rosie snorts and then tilts her head back toward the door. "Down the hall to the left." Then she takes a step closer. "Just *what* kind of a house did you used to work for?"

I shrug. "Oh, it had its charms. Peculiar ones."

TEN

"SHE'LL SEE YOU NOW," Rosie hisses as she bursts through the doorway of her bedroom, where she had left me as soon as the Knights' coach rolled up the street.

Scrambling to my feet, I submit to Rosie's frantic last-minute inspections. Earlier, while the coachman had gone to the station to pick up La Spider and her daughter, Rosie had whipped out a silver needle and thread and basically sewed me into one of Livie's work uniforms. "Let's go," she says at last, as if I'm holding her up, and ducks out the door again. I follow her down the servants' stairway, through the back passages and across the wide marbled foyer, before she brings me to a gilt-edged doorway that leads to Lady Knight's private office. Rosie raises one hand and knocks on the door, then waits.

"Come in," a low voice says. I dig my nails into my palms as Rosie precedes me into the room.

Dark wooden paneling lines the lower half of the walls, while the upper half is covered in a velvety, rich red wallpaper. At one end of the room, a huge fire crackles in the marble fireplace, and at the other end, a woman, seated behind an ornate mahogany desk, is consulting a bound ledger. She doesn't immediately look up at us. So I study the top of her dark head for a while, noting the rich drape of her royal blue skirt, her starched white shirtwaist, and the gleaming ruby earrings. Everything about this room and this woman spells out elegance. Ice cold elegance. Even the fire's heat doesn't seem to be able to penetrate the chill that permeates the air.

La Spider, I think, and almost as if she's heard me, she finally raises her head. Her eyes are two diamonds of light in a carved alabaster face. As they probe into me, I do my best to stand straight and tall and not run away screaming. This woman radiates a tremendous sense of Talent, so palpable that even ordinary people must somehow perceive it. I don't even get this sense from my grandmother, and she's the most powerful witch I can think of. Then her searchlight eyes shift to Rosie and she moves her chin a fraction of an inch downward. Only then does the other girl speak in the most demure voice I've heard from her.

"Lady Knight, this is Agatha Smithsdale. She's come about the position of lady's maid to Lady Jessica."

In a precise voice, La Spider says, "That will be all, Rosie. Tell Cook I'll want to see her next."

"Yes, my lady," Rosie says, and with a swirl of her skirt, she's gone.

I swallow and raise my eyes, even though my eyelids feel like two slabs of stone.

La Spider studies me in silence for a while, her mouth an implacable line. "I assume Rosie has told you everything you need to know about this position. The salary is twelve dollars a month, and you'll have a half day off each week and one full day off each month." She pauses, so I nod. An irritated expression crosses her face and I wonder how many times she has recited this spiel. "I do not know the kind of household you're used to, but in this house, you will be expected to present a neat, clean appearance at all times and to always be available when my daughter or I call for you."

"Yes, my lady," I manage to murmur.

"I wanted a French maid for my daughter. But you're American. You have no references," she says suddenly, and the swift conversational veer startles me even though I was expecting this. "That is most unusual and would not, generally, be acceptable."

"I—"

She tilts her head and I fall silent. "My son, Liam, has vouched for you." And now her lip curls. "I have no idea what gutter he might have found you in. All I know is that you're here and you at least *look* respectable."

For once in my life, I decide sarcasm probably isn't the best idea here. "Thank you, my lady," I say, biting the inside of my cheek to keep any inflection from creeping into my voice.

She stares at me in silence for another moment. "In this house, you will do your work. You will not speak about anyone in this house to anyone *outside* of this house. Instead, you will keep your mouth shut at all times. I can be a fair mistress. I can be a very unforgiving one as well. Is that clear?"

I nod, privately wondering if the other girls got this speech and how hard up they must have been to keep from running out the front door the first second they could. And then I realize that there's no way Livie would have ever dared to steal anything from this woman and expect to live another day. Three minutes in this woman's presence is more than enough confirmation of Cook's words and more than enough proof that Horace and Rosie lied about my predecessor.

And suddenly that's all. She returns to examining the ledger on her desk and I almost collapse with relief to be free of her terrifying gaze. "You may go," she says.

I curtsy, but she doesn't seem to notice. It's as if I've faded into the wallpaper. "Yes, my lady," I say again.

I have a feeling that I'll be saying that a lot.

I close the door softly behind me and take a deep breath, wondering when my heart will resume its normal rate again. Then a burst of wild giggling makes me forget all about the last five minutes.

"Oh, sir, you really do know how to sweep a girl off her feet." Rosie's voice is high and light and airy, as if she's imitating someone. After tiptoeing down the hallway, I stop in front of a partially open door and peer in.

Mr. Tynsdell is waltzing Rosie across what appears to be a salon stuffed with couches and tables. As I watch, they narrowly miss crashing into a lamp and then a side table before whirling past the small piano. Rosie's head is tipped back, her blond hair is flying loose, and her mouth is a bright red circle of laughter as Mr. Tynsdell waggles his eyebrows and contorts his lips into what to me seem like frightening grimaces. But Rosie only shrieks with delight as they collapse into a heap on the gold braided rug by the fireplace.

"Stop, stop," she giggles, twisting her head sideways as he nuzzles his face to hers, sniffing her like a dog. Finally, they sit up and she runs her hands over her hair. In a matter of seconds, she is smoothing away errant strands, tucking everything back neatly under her cap.

Rosie and Mr. Tynsdell?

"That should teach you a lesson," Mr. Tynsdell says, his eyebrows jumping up and down again. It's almost as if he's . . . parodying himself.

And then a chill passes over me.

That isn't Mr. Tynsdell at all.

Before I can test my theory, Rosie says, "Oh, sir, I do love when you chastise me so." She bats her eyelashes at him and as he angles his body closer to hers, she giggles. "Please. I can't kiss him. Not even for you."

Mr. Tynsdell draws back, jutting out his lower lip as if she slapped him. "I knew your love was only surface deep," he says in that deep, sonorous voice.

"You know that's not so," she murmurs, leaning toward him.

Just then a bell rings sharply throughout the room. Rosie scrambles to her feet, shaking out her skirts. "Your mother," she says in a completely different voice. She blows a kiss to the butler and darts toward the fireplace. Frowning, I watch as she ducks behind a floor-to-ceiling tapestry depicting what looks like a hunting party chasing a bright gold unicorn through a deep and gloomy forest. There is a soft grating noise and then silence.

Mr. Tynsdell climbs slowly to his feet and dances a little jig before a gray mist rises from the center of his chest.

Liam steps from the butler's body as neatly as if he's walking through a doorway. Instantly, Mr. Tynsdell's body collapses like a marionette whose strings have just been snipped.

"Are you all right, old chap?" Liam says in his regular voice. "Shall I get some help?"

Mr. Tynsdell looks up at him as if peering through a fog. He blinks, blinks again, and tries to scramble to his feet. I bite my lower lip. He hasn't been exactly nice to me, but there's something horrible about witnessing his lost expression and slackened features.

And there's something even more horrible about the

smirk curling across Liam's face. Knotting my fingers into fists, I wish for the seventeenth time that I hadn't lost my ability to throw fire. Because the whole place would be an inferno right about now.

"I'm sorry, sir. I must have . . . fainted?" Mr. Tynsdell says, and there's weariness in his voice.

"Working too hard, most likely," Liam says. "I'll have a word with your employers," he adds, and then bursts into laughter. Mr. Tynsdell smiles weakly as if he's heard this one before. They both start toward the door.

I zip down the hallway and dart into the next room, praying that it's empty. Fortunately, it is. I seem to have landed in a library. Three of the walls are lined with bookshelves. The fourth contains yet another massive fireplace, which is flanked on either side by more floor-to-ceiling tapestries. Any other time, I would stop to examine the books on the shelves, all of them first editions no doubt, but now I press my ear to the closed door and wait until a thick silence is on the other side. Then I peek out. The hallway is empty. Inching the door open, I slip back into the salon that Liam and Mr. Tynsdell have just left. All of my focus is on the tapestry where Rosie disappeared.

I regard the pale gold unicorn with sympathy, noting the cruel twisted expression embroidered on each hunter's face before lifting the edge of the tapestry and slipping behind it the way Rosie did. The smell of old wool is suddenly overpowering. As a sneeze starts to build somewhere in the back of my nose, I stretch my fingers out in the pitch black and encounter what feels like a wooden panel. A door of some kind. I push inward and it gives beneath my hand. A cool draft of air rushes across my face and I step forward. I wind my way through what feels like a narrow tunnel of dank stone, a soft *drip-drip* batting at my ears until suddenly the space widens into a little square cell. Dim light filters across the flagstone floor, coming from a grate that's set in the wall at about eye level.

After a second I tiptoe forward and press my face against the black bars. I peer out into La Spider's study. I seem to be in a hidden tunnel in the wall opposite to the fireplace. If I angle my body, I can see the spot where I was just standing a few moments ago. And La Spider's profile. She is still sitting in her chair, now writing something swiftly on a square of white paper with a glass pen. I bite my lip. Even though I can't fully see her face, I can tell from the way she holds her head, from the slashing strokes of her arm, from the rigid line of her neck, that she is angry. Deeply angry.

A soft knock comes at the door, and La Spider lifts her head. "Come in," she intones, and from my vantage point I can just see the door handle turn and then a girl enter the room. She advances three paces and then stops. "Mother," the girl says tonelessly.

I examine Jessica Knight with fascination. Apparently, Liam got all the looks in the family, because his sister is small and stocky and her brown hair barely shines at all under the soft glow of the chandelier. Her round face is the color of dirty snow, but I'd bet money that has more to do with the fact that she's standing in front of her mother and less to do with her complexion in general.

"Sit," her mother commands. Before Jessica can respond, an empty chair skids across the room and comes within an inch of slamming into her shins.

Jessica's face blanches to an even less-flattering hue. But then she surprises me by saying, "Will I be allowed to sit of my own volition, or will you cram me into the chair like a doll?"

"Don't try me," La Spider says in that same controlled voice.

Spreading her dark blue skirts gracefully, as if she's just been invited to a tea party, Jessica sits down. Then she lifts her blunt chin and stares pointedly at her mother. I feel an unwilling surge of admiration for her.

"I have just heard that you tried to break off your engagement with Edward Newcastle over the weekend." La Spider's fingers run down the length of her pen.

"How did you hear—? Oh, never mind. I knew you'd find out somehow. Anyway, I succeeded. We won't be married." Jessica's voice is once again devoid of expression, but one hand twitches in her lap.

La Spider pushes back her chair and crosses to a small side table at one edge of the room. She is out of my direct line of sight, but I can hear the faint *chink* of crystal and then the spill of liquid being poured into a glass. Then, with a soft swish of her skirts, she moves back into view holding two glasses full of a dark liquid. The color of rust. Or old blood.

"And why did you attempt to break off the engagement, if I may ask?" Lady Knight says, and holds out one glass to her daughter. Apparently she's decided to ignore her daughter's assertion that she succeeded.

Jessica pauses, then reaches up and takes the glass, but doesn't drink from it. Instead, she focuses on the contents as she smiles slightly. "If you must know, Mother, I find him repulsive. Or maybe I find it repulsive that you so badly want me to marry him." The second time she says *repulsive*, she looks directly up at La Spider, who is still standing over her.

La Spider turns her head and stares at the wall for a second. And then, like a tiny cross bolt, the pen on her desk flies through the air, its sharp tip hovering an inch above Jessica's right eye.

I draw in a shallow breath.

"If you maim me, Mother, how willing do you think anyone will be to marry me? They all want your money, yes, but I doubt that even your wealth will be enough to make a man take on a half-blind wife." Here Jessica lowers her voice to a mock whisper. "Whatever would society say?" Then she gestures at the pen, still hovering above her face, flicking the sharp tip with one finger.

La Spider's lips widen into a red slash of a smile. "Perhaps you're right. But there are other ways to maim you that aren't so visible." The pen zooms downward to the level of Jessica's heart as La Spider strolls back to her desk. "Your music tutor, Mr. Finnegan, appears to be a little lovesick these days."

Jessica freezes in her chair. "I . . . I don't know what you're talking about," she says at last.

"Oh no?" La Spider sets the glass down on her desk, then picks up a small square of cream-colored paper. She dangles it from her fingers as if it's a fish caught on a line. "My dearest Jessica," she begins, her cold voice chipping away at the words. "It is late at night as I write this and all I can think of is you. Your eyes, your—"

"Stop," Jessica shrieks. Her cheeks are two red flags, and she has half risen from her chair.

The pen hovers motionless in the air.

La Spider looks up from the letter, one eyebrow arched. "I must say, Mr. Finnegan is quite . . . ardent."

"How did you get that letter? No one . . . I should have burned it," Jessica finishes at last, sinking back in her seat.

"Do you think you can hide anything from me?" La Spider says, her voice soft and pitying. The pen dances mockingly. "To your health. And to Mr. Finnegan's *continued* health," she adds, then raises her glass and swallows half the contents. She raises one eyebrow again. "You won't drink?"

Jessica examines her own glass. "No, thank you, Mother. I don't care for this . . . vintage that you and Liam seem to love so much."

La Spider shrugs, then drinks again. "I do find that it gives me such a zest for life, such a vitality."

I study Jessica's face. From this distance, I can't tell, but it seems that tears are oozing down her cheeks. "It seems you're running low again, Mother. What next? You can't keep *losing* lady's maids, you know, even if they don't have any family. People will start to talk. Wasn't Livie the fourth one to have disappeared?"

"She wouldn't have died," La Spider says lightly. "Not if you hadn't been so stubborn."

"Stubborn?" Jessica says with a brief laugh.

"Enough," La Spider says. With a swift movement, she flicks the letter into the fireplace. Flames eat the paper within seconds. I watch Jessica's eyes briefly close then open again. Her expression is once again blank, impassive.

"Edward Newcastle will be given to understand that you are a stupid young girl." Here La Spider pauses and looks at her daughter again. "Which is nothing but the truth. He will understand that you were overcome with a fit of nerves and therefore your engagement is back on. *You will not attempt to break it off again.* Is that clear?"

Jessica glances down at the pen, daggerlike, still hovering over her heart. Suddenly, she reaches out, snatches the pen, and with one move rakes the sharp quill tip across her bare arm. Blood boils to the surface of her skin, spills over from the edges of the cut. In a low, emotionless tone, Jessica says, "I wish on all the elements that I could drain this away. Then I would be no different from those ordinary, filthy humans you so love to use."

La Spider gazes at her daughter, her profile serene. "Heal yourself," she says quietly. "Before you ruin my carpet."

Jessica shrugs, and presses her right hand against the seep of blood. Then she takes her hand away, wipes it on her skirt.

La Spider sighs, then says, "Need I remind you that Edward Newcastle is a rising political star? That one day, with our help, he will be the president of this country? Need I remind you of what power that will bring to us all? Any girl would trade places with you in a second."

"They would regret that soon enough," Jessica murmurs, and she closes her eyes as if exhausted. "May I go now?"

"You may," La Spider says, and she turns back to her papers as Jessica shuffles up from her chair. "Oh," La Spider says, and her tone is lighter.

Jessica pauses at the door but doesn't turn back.

"I've hired a new maid for you."

"How long will this one last, I wonder. Until Liam kills her in one of his *experiments*," Jessica says, and I can't decide if I'm more horrified at her words or at the casual tone in which she utters them.

"Well, if he does, we'll just have to find another one," La Spider replies almost absently as she selects another pen and pulls a fresh sheet of writing paper from an ornate golden stand on her desk. Then she lifts her head and stares into the fire. "She has no family, apparently, so that's something. I'll never hire another girl with family. It's *such* a nuisance."

"You mean it's such a nuisance to kill them if the family comes asking questions? Yes, I can see how that could really put you off your dinner, Mother," Jessica comments dryly.

La Spider waves her hand through the air as if swatting a fly and returns her gaze to the desk. Jessica opens her mouth as if she's about to add something else, but then seems to change her mind in favor of pulling open the door and leaving the room.

I press my lips together to keep from screaming. It's very clear why Horace seemed so eager to bring me to Rosie once I told him that I didn't have any family and why Liam seemed so willing to hire me. And why Rosie didn't even care that he was flirting with me in the kitchen.

Until Liam kills her in one of his experiments.

I find myself praying that my borrowed Talent of freezing people doesn't desert me just when I need it the most.

ELEVEN

I HURRY BACK ALONG THE passageway, my hands outstretched like a blind person's until I literally run into the small grated door. Fighting my way free of the smothering wool tapestry, I emerge once again into the salon, which is still thankfully empty. Then I lean against a bookshelf and stare at the empty fireplace. Either Dawn or Lily, the two housemaids, must have scoured it this morning, because not one single speck of ash mars the pristine marble. Restless, I pace to the large multipaned windows that line one side of the room. Dusk is creeping along the sills, edging the frames and gathering under the trees of Madison Square Park. All along the street, gas lamps have flared to life. Most of the din of the street is blocked out, but I can still hear the faint creaking of carriage wheels and a persistent ringing noise, which I pinpoint from a vendor who is lugging a small wagon behind him. Even in the gloom I can make out a brightly painted pair of scissors and a knife on one side of his cart. Every so often he stops, puts his hands to his mouth, and cries out, "Razors, scissors, knives to grind!" I follow his progress up the street, and then my eyes flicker back.

There is a man standing on the street corner opposite the house. Draped in a dark coat, he waits just outside of the circle of light cast by a gas lamp. In the bustling street, he alone is perfectly still. Something about the way he is standing makes me think he's been stationed there for a while. I lean forward, craning my neck, but it's no use. I can't make out his features. My first thought is that it's Alistair. But he's carrying a cane, and also he seems shorter than Alistair, and thicker. Just then he looks up, directly at me. And then suddenly the light from the street lamp winks out.

I back away from the window and sink down into a leather-covered chair. My head is whirling, and when I press my fingers to my eyes, it only makes it worse. Images of La Spider and her flying pen, Jessica's bleeding arm that suddenly wasn't bleeding a minute later, and Mr. Tynsdell spinning Rosie around and around the room and then Liam stepping out of the butler's body all scurry past my eyelids until I feel like my brain is swelling up inside my skull.

"Focus, Tam," I mutter to myself, and the images flicker, then recede. Okay. So far I've discovered that Alistair hasn't arrived yet. Good. That Liam and La Spider are presumably experimenting and killing housemaids and drinking their blood. There's no telling if they're also already controlling humans the way Alistair could control my sister. And presumably they haven't started experimenting on people with Talents.

Yet.

Without realizing it, I've gotten to my feet and have been pacing the length of the library, back and forth. Now more than ever it's crucial to find the Greenes and warn them. Before Alistair visits again.

Gabriel.

On the one hand, I could really use some help right now of the Gabriel kind. On the other hand, if La Spider and Liam get their claws into him . . .

There are other ways to maim you that aren't so visible. La Spider's voice oozes through my head. If she would do that to her own daughter, what wouldn't she do?

Digging my fingers into my temples, I come to a comlete stop by one bookcase-lined wall. "I can't let you," I say as if Gabriel is actually standing in front of me. Rowena probably backed down by now. No, she must have at least tried to use her Talent to compel him to stay in the twenty-first century; otherwise he'd be here already. But she could change her mind at any minute and decide to stop compelling him. *Think, think, think.*

I summon my grandmother's words, trying to take comfort in them. *It's up to you to allow when a person's Talent can work on you and when it can't. It's entirely your choice.* Closing my eyes, I sink inward, pouring all of my Talent into a silent mantra. *Don't find me, don't find me, don't find me. I resist, I resist, I resist.*

I cross to the door with those words echoing through me.

"Wake up, Tam," Agatha's annoyingly cheerful morning voice greets me.

"Ugh," I mumble, and roll away from her hovering presence, pulling my comforter over my head. But then my feet are bare and suddenly freezing and my comforter feels thinner than usual.

"Wake up or you'll be late for your first day," Agatha insists, her voice blurring into the raindrops pattering against the windows. Then the covers are yanked back and a pain twists through my upper arm.

"Ow," I shriek, bolting upright in bed. "What the—"

Rosie is standing over my bed, fully dressed in her black uniform, her face freshly scrubbed and her hair smoothly pinned into a neat chignon.

I rub my arm, staring at the red marks on my skin. "Thanks," I mutter.

She shrugs. "You don't want to be late on your first day. Lady Jessica will want her morning chocolate in fifteen minutes and you'd better be ready."

Sighing, I put my feet on the floor, then immediately

retract them to the scant warmth of the bed. Apparently, rich nineteenth-century employers don't believe in a trivial thing like heat in the servants' quarters. I blink up at Rosie's unsympathetic face and then across at her neatly made bed. Her neatly made, clearly unslept-in-all-night bed.

After stumbling to the dresser, I pick up the white enameled pitcher and slop a few inches of water into the wide-lipped basin. I set the pitcher back down on the dresser, and then there's no more delaying. I plunge my hands into the ice water and splash my face once, twice. Gasping for breath, I reach for the thin cotton towel that seems incapable of drying anything. I scrub at my face with it, more to get the blood circulating than anything else, and then yawn my way into my clothes.

Through all this Rosie watches me impassively, and finally, when I present myself to her, she nods once. "Twenty minutes after you bring Lady Jessica her morning chocolate, you will come back and help her get dressed. She has a music lesson at a quarter to ten in the drawing room, so a shirtwaist and her blue poplar skirt will do. Then she is to take lunch with the Ladies Auxiliary Charity, so she'll need to dress in a gray wool, most likely. Then she'll go coaching in the afternoon and perhaps a bit of shopping, so her gray wool with her scarlet cape and fur muff for that, and then tonight is their night at the theater . . . Are you listening to all of this?" Rosie plunks one hand on her hip.

But I can't help it. My eyes have wandered to our little dormer window, checking the street corner where that man was standing the night before. Pieces of last night's dreams trickle through my head.

"Agatha!"

I straighten to attention. "Yeah—yes. Gray wool, fur muff, blue poplar, got it. Music lesson, charity lunch, coaching, shopping, theater." Sounds like a rough life.

Rosie gives me a look. "I'll manage," I say to her now. She rolls her eyes and I decide to refrain from asking her just when is my day off.

It doesn't seem like exactly the right moment for that question.

Getting through Jessica's door while balancing a large tray with a cup, a saucer, and a full pot of hot chocolate, not to mention a basket full of bread and dishes of butter and jam, is no small feat. But I manage, even though the pot lurches once and the cup rattles in its saucer.

"Good morning, Lady Jessica," I say in a singsong voice that I imagine a lady's maid would use. I figure I might as well play my part to the fullest. I glance toward the bed, expecting to see her blinking sleepily at me. But the bed is empty. Instead, she is standing by the fire, which Dawn or Lily must have lit earlier this morning. And she's fully dressed. Okay, good, that makes my job easier, since I was wondering how to deal with all the little hooks and buttons and thingies.

Setting down the tray on a small side table, I say, "I'm your new—"

"Yes. I know who you are. Agatha Smiterdone." Her fingers clutch a piece of paper.

"Smithsdale," I interject, but she barely nods. She strides toward the fire, then whirls suddenly and comes toward me. I step back. It's hard to reconcile this girl with the one I saw in her mother's study. She is full of restless movements and a sharp, jumbling energy. Stopping a few feet away from me, she studies my face intently. I wait for the prickle across my skin to let me know that she's trying to use her Talent on me, but I feel nothing. Besides, it seems her Talent is being able to heal, so unless she wants to fix the scrape on my thumb that I just got when trying to open the door, there's not much else she could do.

"I need your help," she says finally.

I blink. "Of course, my lady. Would you like to change your dress or . . . your hairstyle?" I finish weakly, examining the sloppy bun Jessica's pulled her hair into. Definitely not one of the hairstyles Rosie taught me.

She shakes her head, although she does put one hand up to her hair as if to check that it's still piled on her head. "I need to leave the house. Without anyone noticing."

"Oh," I say, more interested now. I glance toward the

door, which I managed to shut with my hip. "But your music lesson starts in—"

She fans away my words by waving the piece of paper through the air. "I canceled it. Unbeknownst to my mother."

"What would you like me to do?" I say carefully, trying to ignore the wisps of buttery-smelling steam that curl up from the breadbasket on the table. When I stumbled into the kitchen, Mr. Tynsdell informed me in a pinched voice that I was too late for breakfast and needed to get these things up to Lady Jessica in a hurry.

"I'll be leaving the house by the side entrance. I need you to go ahead of me and let me know if the way is clear. And then" —she takes a tremulous breath— "and then, I'll need a chaperone. I'll need you to come with me . . ." Her words trail away and she blinks rapidly. Then she recovers and adds, "Simple enough?"

It doesn't really sound like a question.

I nod, watch as she gathers up a little black purse and a shawl and bustles toward the door.

"Oh, and Agatha?" she says when we're at the door. "I know servants like to gossip, but truly, if you mention this to anyone . . ." She narrows her eyes at me.

Suddenly, I get the oddest feeling that she's been practicing these words in front of her mirror all morning. I try to look suitably intimidated. "Of course not, my lady," I murmur.

She bites her lip, then nods once and motions for me to step ahead of her.

We skim along the silent hallway of the second floor, our footsteps swallowed up by the thick maroon carpeting, and hurry down the wide staircase. So far, so good. As we cross the gold and white foyer, gleaming in the morning sunshine, the light sound of laughter spills from the door to our left.

"Mother's entertaining the ladies from her club," Jessica mutters. "She can't stand them, but . . . keep going," she hisses at me as I pause.

Finally, we reach the side door. Motioning for me to go first, Jessica falls in behind me, so close that she's breathing on my neck. "All clear?" she whispers, and I nod once and we slip out the door, shutting it behind us with barely a sound.

"Where are we going?" I ask a little breathlessly as Jessica cuts up an alleyway and then darts across the street, narrowly avoiding two horse-drawn carriages.

"To the circus," she gasps back.

"Step up, step up, step up, ladies and gentlemen, one and all," bawls a man in a dark suit. He is standing on a milk crate, and above him hangs a bright banner. THE ONE AND ONLY TIMMONS FAMILY CIRCUS is spelled out in curling blue and gold letters. The man's hands move in a blur, exchanging bills and coins and tickets as Jessica comes to a halt.

She turns her head rapidly, scanning the crowds, and then goes very still and she seems to stare at a tall young man dressed in a black suit. He has taken his bowler hat off and is fanning his face with it even though there's already a brisk wind blowing.

"Mr. Finnegan," Jessica calls in a high voice, and I recall the name that La Spider threw at her in the study.

"Jessica," the man says, and comes toward us at a half run. "I almost thought you weren't coming."

"I wasn't going to," she says stiffly, her face slightly averted. "But your letter . . . I . . . Here," she says, and abruptly thrusts her closed fist toward him. A bewildered expression crosses his face and then he reaches out. A little cameo pin winks from her hand into his.

"I . . . don't understand."

"But you do," she says, gazing at him steadily now. "It's over, William. I can't indulge this any longer."

"If it's your family, I . . ."

"I'm engaged to be married." The words seem chiseled out of stone.

"But you said you'd break it off." His voice trails away as he studies her set features. He pauses for a moment, his eyes skipping over me, and I look down at my feet. "At least, Jessica, let me take you to the circus. For one hour. It's all I ask. Please," he whispers as she opens her mouth again.

The smell of sawdust and sweat fills the air, as well as the scent of something burning. Glancing sideways, I watch as a half-naked man painted in blue symbols swallows a whole torch full of fire to the accompaniment of gasps from the crowd. I really hope the burning smell isn't coming from him.

"One hour," she says finally. "Agatha will accompany us," she adds with a jerk of her head.

"I could just wait here for you, my lady," I say desperately. In one hour, I could ask at least one hundred people if they know the Greenes.

"No," Jessica says coldly.

For a second I think about walking away. What could she do to me? I'm not here in 1887 just to brush hair and pick out ball gowns. And then I remember Alistair will inevitably return to the Knight house. If I can stop him from ever reaching La Spider, that's accomplishing something.

I nod and fall in three paces behind them as they head toward the ticket line. They'd better be buying me a ticket.

Once inside the small park, I follow at a discreet distance, sidestepping hordes of people. I've figured out that we're just a few blocks south and east of Hell's Kitchen, which happens to be the home of one of my favorite flea markets. But judging from the pretty shabbily dressed people and the rows and rows of warehouses and shacks lining the park—okay, *park* is stretch: a small green space—it's not quite yet the neighborhood that I know.

A group of children is gathered in front of a small ring

where an elephant, tethered to a stake by one foot, is sitting back on its hind legs, almost like a person. A pink and white teacup is cradled in its trunk, and as the children watch, it raises and lowers its trunk as if drinking.

"How charming," Jessica cries, her voice light and happy. She flings her arm out, tugging on Mr. Finnegan's sleeve, and they stop to watch as the elephant accepts a slice of bread from its handler, tucking it carefully into its gaping mouth.

As the crowd claps enthusiastically, my eyes are drawn upward to the small tree, which offers a little shade on the dusty clearing. A large black crow perches on an overhanging branch, its head cocked, its yellow glass eyes pinned to the scene below. Its very stillness seems off somehow, and I stare at it for so long that I look away just in time to see Jessica and Mr. Finnegan moving toward the striped tent along with another wave of people. As I hurry after them, I glance back once. The crow glides silently off the branch, circles once, and settles on the round dome of the striped tent. It points its beak downward and stares at me.

That does it. I reach out with my mind and *pull* hard.

With a startled squawk, the crow bursts into flight, then half falls, half flies down the side of the tent to the ground. In a millisecond the bird's form blurs and lengthens. I find myself now staring at a girl my age, her long red hair loose over her shoulders. She glares up at me as I take three steps closer. Just then a small child blunders into my side, his outstretched finger pointing toward the girl on the ground.

"Mama, Mama," he babbles. "That lady. She was a bird. She—"A woman wearing a patched blue dress, with another infant locked under her arm, reaches down and gives the boy a slap across his ear. His words abruptly transform into a shriek.

"Don't run off like that," she says, giving me a harried look. "Begging your pardon, miss," she mutters, and then tugs her wailing child away.

"But she was a bird," he sobs again.

I turn back to find that the girl has climbed to her feet and is brushing the dust off her plain gray dress. Her hair tumbles forward over her shoulders. Her skin, lightly freckled, is flushed either with heat or emotion.

"Who are you?" I say immediately.

She cocks her head at me, studies me with green-gold eyes. "I could ask you the same thing," she says at last.

"I saw you turn from a crow into a girl."

She shifts her shoulders. "Are you sure about that? Appearances can be deceiving." But a thread of curiosity or fear is running under her light words, and her eyes never stop examining my face.

I hesitate, wanting to ask her if she is connected in any way to the man who I saw standing on the street corner. Then I blurt out, "Are you from the Greene family?"

She doesn't answer and her face doesn't change, but her upper body inclines back just a degree.

"You are, aren't you?" I take a step closer. "Please, I need to see you. All of you. It's urgent. You're in danger."

The girl's eyes narrow. "You come here with Jessica Knight and you want to warn me about danger. The others don't trust you. *A stranger will come from a faraway time, bringing the end of our days as we know them.*"

"That's Alistair, not me!" I practically scream at her.

"Alistair?" the girl asks.

"You read that in the book, right?" I try to remember the exact wording that both my grandmother and Rowena had read. "Doesn't it say that a stranger comes to town in the dying days of the year? And that he knows much more than he should. He? Him? It's a *man*. His name's Alistair Knight."

But she is shaking her head. "Only a stranger, seen entering the house of the Knights. And that death and destruction follow her."

"That's not right," I whisper. And then I remember my sister warning me just how hard it was to read the book, to make even a few words appear. Apparently, these Greenes have only seen that a stranger was coming. "Please. I have to meet your family. Where do you live? Just tell me that much."

"Agatha," Jessica calls, and I want to scream at the other girl's timing. When I don't turn immediately, Jessica calls again, "Agatha." This time her voice is sharp and precise, a faint echo of La Spider's. I turn to see Jessica and Mr. Finnegan standing at the tent entrance. Mr. Finnegan looks confused, while Jessica's eyes are burning. She lifts her chin in what appears to be a nod, but the gesture is not aimed at me.

I glance back at the crow girl, who has now moved a few steps away, her face a shuttered window. She inclines her head back at Jessica and then her eyes flick back to my face. "I'll find you again."

Before I can answer, she slips off into the crowd.

Turning, I walk back to Jessica, who immediately hisses, "What did she say to you?" Her eyes are narrowed, and suddenly her resemblance to her mother is striking.

I do my best to appear confused. "The young lady? I stepped on her foot so I was apologizing to her," I explain swiftly, hoping that Jessica didn't see the girl change from a bird. "Do you know her?" I ask now. "I didn't mean any harm, my lady, I just—"

"Never mind," Jessica says shortly, and turns back to Mr. Finnegan.

The rest of the hour passes in a blur. I barely take in the trapeze artists and the prancing horses and the lion tamers. Instead, I keep a respectable three feet behind Jessica and Mr. Finnegan. *"I'll find you again." Please, please, please let her be telling the truth.*

"Where to now?" Mr. Finnegan is saying, gesturing

with his free arm toward the wide swath of green tents that we haven't yet entered. But Jessica shakes her head, biting down on her lower lip.

"I have to go," she says at last. "They'll already be wondering where I am, and—"

"It's not been an hour yet," Mr. Finnegan says, but still she pulls herself free.

Her shoulders curve downward. "It doesn't matter," she says at last. "An hour, a week, a year—none of it makes any difference." Then she straightens up, takes three steps toward me. "Come, Agatha. We're going back."

I nod, trying not to notice how crushed Mr. Finnegan looks.

"Jessica," he says softly, catching at her hand. "Please—"

"It's over, William," she says, her voice flat. "Once and for all. Please don't contact me again."

"Then keep this," he murmurs, and swiftly presses the brooch back into her hand. "To remember me."

She nods once, then walks away from him, her back held in a needle-straight line.

I throw an awkward half smile at William. *Believe me, you're better off far away from these people.* I almost tell him that. But I decide to play lady's maid just a little longer and follow Jessica instead.

Jessica is silent as we slip back through the crowded streets, her face carefully blank, and I realize she is assembling her mask again. The change from the giddy and laughing girl of half an hour ago is startling.

I'm reminded of how I used to assemble my very own such armor anytime I walked into my house at Hedgerow. Before I knew I had a Talent, when I thought I had no place in my own family. The idea that Jessica Knight and I could have anything in common is so weird that I'm almost grateful to the horse-drawn truck that is barreling down on us, as it provides a welcome distraction from that uncomfortable thought.

Finally, we turn off Madison and reach the relative quiet of Twenty-seventh Street with its pristine rows of brownstones. Storm clouds are now scuttling across the sky, and the breeze has picked up, outlining our legs through our skirts. Jessica and I approach the side entrance cautiously, but no one seems around at this hour. Looking up, I pinpoint two birds perched on the gabled window of the neighboring house. I reach out and tug at them, but nothing happens. They're only birds.

"This household is . . . very different from your last, I imagine," she says finally as we reach the black gate.

"All households are different," I say neutrally. I glance over my shoulder, but except for a few strollers and a woman pushing a pram, the street is still. No crows perched in any of the trees.

Then I gaze sideways at Jessica, who still has made no move to go inside the gate.

Instead, her eyes are filling with tears and her fingers are clutching convulsively around the little cameo pin. Before I can think of what to say, she blinks once, twice, and then her calm veneer shifts back into place. "Here," she blurts out, and presses the cameo into my hand.

I stare down at the woman's engraved face, at the tendrils of hair that curl against her ivory neck. Without thinking, I press the side of the pin, and the face slides open to reveal a small watch inside. A steady ticking, almost too soft to hear, brushes at my ears.

"It's sweet, isn't it?" Jessica murmurs, her eyes downcast. "It must have taken a month's wages for him to buy it."

"Are you sure you—"

"Keep it," she murmurs. "And take my advice," she says softly. "Leave this house. As soon as you can." And with that she slips into the side gate, leaving me no choice but to follow her.

Somehow I manage to get through the rest of the day without any major mistakes. True, Jessica wrenched a petticoat away from me when I fumbled the laces, but other than that she was silent as I helped her get ready for her afternoon of coaching with whomever she was supposed to do that with. In fact, I started to think of her as a human-size doll that I had to dress up in different outfits, even though I kind of always hated dolls when I was little.

Now, after an excruciatingly early dinner with Rosie,

Cook, and Mr. Tynsdell, who glared at me every time I raised the fork to my mouth, I am sitting in the tiny upstairs room wondering what to do with the rest of the evening and the night ahead of me. Jessica already told me not to wait up for her. "I don't need any help this evening," she added, probably because I looked startled. I kept my mouth shut and nodded because I had no idea that a lady's maid was supposed to wait up.

Darkness presses close against the little dormer window and the wind buffets against the glass panes. A chill seeps into the room. Shivering, I cross to the window and stare out at the street. Carriages are rolling across the cobblestones, the faint clatter rising to meet my ears. All sorts of people are bustling across the streets, lingering to talk to each other in twos or threes despite the cold November evening.

"Thinking of jumping?" Rosie says behind me, and I do jump, smacking my head against the glass.

I glare at her, but she laughs. Her cheeks are tinged pink and her hair is loosened a little. "Where did you go after dinner?" I ask, but she only winks at me.

"Can't know all my secrets, Agatha!" she says gaily. Crossing to the cracked mirror above our dresser, she gazes into it while pulling back her hair into a smooth knot. She reaches into her drawer, withdraws a little pot, and dusts something onto her forehead and nose. The sweet smell of talcum powder flitters into the air between us, and suddenly,

I swallow hard and for one instant envision myself back in my dorm room at school with the real Agatha as we both glitter ourselves up for a night out in the city.

"Don't wait up for me," Rosie says, snapping shut the lid of her box. Then with a wink she slips out of the room.

I wait for the space of one heartbeat, and then ease off my shoes. On cat-soft feet I follow her. Thankfully, Lady Knight doesn't seem to believe in wasting lamp oil on her servants, so plenty of thick shadows line the walls. I melt into them as I pad down the servants' back staircase, letting Rosie dash ahead of me.

When I reach the landing, I expect her to continue down the three curving flights to the kitchen, but halfway there, she disappears. Or actually, I can't hear her anymore. I press into the side wall and wait, listening as hard as I can. I've noticed that the door to the kitchen always squeaks a little, so I wait for that familiar sound. But there is only silence.

And then a soft *snick* whispers across the landing below me.

I follow the curve of the spiral of the stairs as fast as I can, only to find more shadows and one lamp casting a feeble flickering light across the thin red carpet of this landing. On impulse, I reach up and unhook the lantern from its iron wall sconce. The oil sputters and hisses with the motion, then settles, and the flame burns true.

Okay, so not the kitchen. The only other option is back

the way I came. I climb up the stairs again, retracing my steps, swinging the lantern this way and that. I have to do this three times before I see it. Right under the third bend in the staircase is a small door. Even with the light of the oil lamp I can just make out the three simple lines of its frame that is perfectly flush with the wall. And now I come to my next problem. There's no doorknob.

Running my free hand along the panels that blend into the wall gives me nothing. I press the wood where the doorknob would be, but still nothing. I lean back a little and study the door again, that soft *snick* echoing in my ears.

The lamp sputters again in my hand, and I look at it thoughtfully. Then I turn and examine the wall behind me. Another iron wall sconce—only this one is empty. Stretching my arm, I nestle the lamp securely into the wall sconce and am rewarded with that same soft *snick*.

I turn back and confront the wall. The door has slid back and become a gaping mouth that leads into another tunnel.

I step into the doorway, reach up, and brush both hands along the walls on either side of me. My right hand encounters nothing but cobwebs and something slimy that scuttles away from me. I stifle a scream, and just then my left hand skims across a small switch. The door suddenly slides shut behind me, leaving me in complete blackness.

Great.

I step forward, feeling my way slowly, wishing that

I had brought my shoes after all. The dampness of hard stone seeps through my stockings and worms into the soles of my feet. The passageway slopes down after a second, and I stumble but catch myself against one wall. Cautiously navigating the steps that I seem to have found, I wind downward in the dark. After a while a faint light begins to grow before me, and then at the level of my ankles I see a square grate, about two feet tall and a foot wide, full of a flickering light.

Crouching down on my heels, I peer out into a room that looks like a study, with books and tables and one desk against the wall. I haven't seen this room before. Judging from the distance I've traveled, I'm guessing it's somewhere on the second floor. A fire is burning steadily in the massive fireplace directly across from my grate, but the crack of wood is the only noise in the room. That, and a soft ticking coming from a clock hanging on the same wall as the fireplace.

The clock that Alistair once asked me to find back when I thought he was merely a professor at NYU.

The clock that Gabriel and I Traveled back to 1899 to steal.

TWELVE

CHEWING MY LIP, I LEAN BACK against the wall, not caring about potential crawly things. Instead, I run through my options. Destroying the clock now won't help. My family—in this century—still apparently needs it for the spell that they will eventually cast on the Knight family. Stealing it to bring to the nineteenth-century Greenes might work. If I could even find them. This can't be where Rosie vanished to unless there's a door that I haven't come across yet. Besides, the passageway runs on and I have a feeling it branches out through the rest of the house. Shifting, I am about to climb to my feet when the door suddenly opens and Mr. Tynsdell enters followed by a tall man wrapped in a dark overcoat. Raindrops gleam across the man's glasses and on the brim of his black bowler hat, which he holds in both hands.

Alistair.

Suddenly, I'm glad that I'm sitting down in this

cramped passageway, as I don't think my knees would have supported my standing weight.

"If you'll just wait here, sir, I'll see if Master Liam is even at home. This isn't the customary hour for calls," Mr. Tynsdell says, his voice peevish with reproof.

"I understand that only too well." Alistair breaks off his words in ragged chunks. "But they need to know that this is *urgent*."

I close my eyes, hearing the echo of that same word that I threw at the crow girl this afternoon.

"Find someone. Lady Knight, Master Liam—anyone," Alistair says, gesturing sharply with his hat. He looks as if he's about to start beating Mr. Tynsdell across the face with it, and the butler seems to realize this. He steps back and eyes Alistair for a moment.

"As I've told you, sir: Lady Knight is not at home. She has gone to the theater."

"What theater?" Alistair asks wildly, hope blustering across his face.

"I wouldn't know," Mr. Tynsdell says, his voice solidifying into a vast and icy wilderness. "I will see if Master Liam is even available." And with that he pivots neatly and leaves the room.

Alistair heaves out a sigh and begins pacing, in and out of my line of vision.

Think, think, think, Tamsin. But short of prying the grate loose and then bashing Alistair over the head with it, I don't know what to do. Then a spark of an idea comes to me. If I can just get in there, freeze Alistair, and then somehow drag him back into the passageway with me, I can prevent this meeting from ever taking place. I arch up and begin skimming my hands over the wall in increasingly desperate swoops, searching for a way into the room.

But then the door to the study opens again and Mr. Tynsdell reenters. My small flare of hope is smothered as Liam appears behind the butler. "Mr. Knight, this is . . . Mr. Callum. Mr. Callum, this is Mr. Knight." Mr. Tynsdell pauses, then asks, "Shall I bring any claret, sir?"

Liam raises his eyebrows at Alistair and says in a hearty tone, "How about it? You look like you could use a drink."

I study Alistair, acknowledging that Liam is right. Alistair does look like a man in need of a drink. Or in need of something. His skin has taken on a grayish tone and even from my limited vantage point I can pick out the half-moon-shaped bruises under his eyes. He looks like . . . Rowena when she was sick. When he was draining her blood and drinking it himself. Either he's already feeling the effects of Traveling that Rowena warned about or it's an addiction that needs to be fed. Or both.

Alistair hesitates, moistens his lips with the point of his tongue, then shakes his head. Liam gives a *suit yourself* type of shrug, and then with a motion of his hand indicates that Mr. Tynsdell should depart. The door closes again and the two men regard each other.

"Liam," Alistair says, his voice cracking now. He takes a step forward and reaches out one hand in an almost child-ish gesture.

But Liam shifts back. "I didn't give you leave to call me by my first name." His voice is still polite, but a note of warning flickers under it.

Alistair checks his forward motion, his hand curling through empty air. "No, no, of course not. Forgive me. Your customs are not known to me. Let me start again. I want to tell you my name. My *real* name. I have waited so long to use it." Then, as if he can't contain the flurry of words, he adds, "I've waited so long to see you and your mother."

"Yes," Liam says now in a bored voice. "Mr. Tynsdell mentioned you had called before. Listen, if it's for one of those charities, my mother already gives more than—"

"It is not for charity." Alistair's voice is sharp. "I am not here because of a *charity*. I am not like the rest of them." And here he flings one arm out as if indicating a crowd of starving beggars. *"I am one of you."*

"How so?" Liam asks softly. He has withdrawn to the fireplace and now selects a poker from the rack of iron tools. He plunges the tip of it into a burning log, which hisses and then snaps into a thousand sparks.

"My name is Alistair Knight," Alistair says quietly to Liam's broad back. "I am related to you and I have come to warn you. I have Traveled a long way. Do you understand me?"

At this Liam turns slowly, the poker dangling from his fingertips. "You've *Traveled*, did you say?"

"Yes."

Liam's eyebrows point upward in an expression of wonder. "No one in our family is able to do that. Is that your Talent?" His voice takes on a note that I can only identify as hunger.

Alistair pauses. "No," he concedes. "I Traveled with the help of a device called the Domani. A device that you need to demolish before it even exists."

I press cold fingers to my mouth, my eyes drifting over to the small wall clock that is steadily ticking away the minutes, the seconds, that my family has to survive. But Alistair seems too bent on speaking to notice its presence in the room.

"My dear man, you're raving," Liam says, and now he's forced good humor into his tone, the way someone would when talking to a child.

Hope blooms again in me. Maybe Liam will think Alistair's crazy and leave it at that.

"I am not *raving*," Alistair says, and something about his tone must have set Liam on edge, because I watch as the other man's nostrils flare once. "I have Traveled from a future where we don't exist. All of our Talents have been stripped away. We're *ordinary*."

"And how does this even come to pass?" Liam asks now, taking a step closer.

"The Greene family," Alistair says. "They—"

But whatever else he was going to say about my family is cut off by Liam's great shout of laughter.

"The Greene family, did you say? That pitiful bunch of pig farmers?"

I frown. Pig farmers? My mother was sort of vague on what the family was doing in New York City during this century, but I didn't think we were living in the city raising pigs.

Evidently, Alistair is confused also. "They're not to be dismissed. Even now they're plotting to—"

"Cera Greene and her bunch of useless sisters and brothers? They're nothing. No one of any consequence in society."

"But they will be, don't you see? They know what you're up to and they'll—"

"And what are we up to?" Liam asks, still smiling.

Here Alistair hesitates, and then his hands unfurl. Taking a step forward, he says, "The experiments on humans and eventually on those with Talents. Learning that we can extend our life span and also our own Talents and the control of others who have them."

"And just what is your Talent?" Liam asks suddenly.

Alistair frowns and I lean forward. My foot slides against the rough stone floor, making the slightest of scraping noises. Alistair turns his head, his gaze stabbing in my direction. "Yes," he whispers hoarsely. At the same time I feel a tingling pass over my skin, followed swiftly by that sharp mental clarity that comes whenever someone tries to use a Talent against me.

I close my eyes in relief. Whatever he just tried to do my Talent blocked.

But now Alistair is frowning even more, and I realize that he is puzzled.

"It just revealed itself to me when I arrived. Because I now exist in a time before . . . before the Greenes steal our powers."

Liam sucks in a breath. "And what is it?"

Alistair licks his dried-out lips. "I can see through walls, through barriers."

"Fascinating," Liam murmurs, leaning the poker against the side of the hearth. "I think I'd like to try that for myself." All at once he shimmers and dissolves into a gray mist that gathers itself into a pulsing ball. It hovers for a second in the air and then swoops into Alistair's chest. At the same time, Alistair makes a strangled sound while clutching at his heart. He closes his eyes, then opens them again and takes a few steps around the room, his hands outstretched, like a toddler learning to walk. Then Alistair/Liam swings his head sharply and focuses on the walls.

Without thinking, I reach out with my mind and block whatever he's about to try.

Do it again, I beg Alistair/Liam silently. *One more time and it's mine.* But after a moment, Alistair/Liam shrugs and then Alistair's body ripples and shudders before crumpling to the floor. One hand spasms on the carpet and then stills. A gray mist pours out of Alistair's chest and reforms into Liam, who steps over Alistair's prone body with care. Liam shakes himself a little, like a dog shaking itself free of raindrops, and stares down at Alistair's body.

"What did you . . . what did you do to me?" Alistair murmurs from the floor.

"A little experiment. I didn't manage to see through any walls, though, old chap. I think you might be wrong about that." Liam wanders back over to the fireplace, picks up the poker again, and examines the fire as if deciding where to poke it next.

"She's here," Alistair says, and if possible, his face goes even whiter. He sits up with a lurch. "She's in this house somewhere," he says urgently to Liam. "Tamsin Greene."

"Who?" Liam says.

Alistair's mouth works. "She . . . I know she's here."

"Now you really are raving, my good man." Liam studies the poker, running one finger along its wrought-iron handle. "Still," he says, so softly that I have to strain to hear him. "Still . . . you might prove useful. You might allow me the means to achieve what I need. You see, my mother's rather against me experimenting on our own family, but she might make an exception for you. Seeing as you're . . . a more distant relation, shall we say?"

"Yes," Alistair breathes, fastening his eyes on Liam's face. "That's what I want. That's what I'm meant to do. I can help you."

"I'm so glad to hear you say that," Liam murmurs.

And all at once, in a motion almost too swift for me to follow, he swings up the poker and brings it down against the back of Alistair's skull.

THIRTEEN

JUST IN TIME I PRESS MY LIPS together to keep from screaming. I want to block out this sight, but it's as if my eyelids have been glued open.

Liam steps back and then plunges the poker into the fire again as if shifting logs is his only concern. After the fire has scoured the poker clean he sets it back in the rack. Only then does he turn and, taking an empty crystal goblet from his desk, stoops by Alistair's motionless body, pressing the goblet to Alistair's ear. Horrified, I watch as the crystal cup fills with blood. When the glass is almost full Liam sets it on the desk and wipes his hands with a handkerchief he procures from his pocket. Sighing, he stares down at the stained cloth for a moment and then tosses it into the fire, where it flares a second later. Then he crosses to the doorway and presses a small black button.

A minute later, there's a knock on the door and Rosie enters. But she's not alone. She's holding the hand of a very small child. From the pants and shirt, I'm guessing it's a boy, although I can't quite tell between the smudges of dirt on its face and the cap on its head. "I brought him like you asked. Found this one in the usual place. Five Points. He—"

"Did anyone see you?" Liam interrupts.

She tosses her head. "Do you think I'm new at this?" she asks with a grin. And then the pleased expression fades from her face as Liam steps back and she sees Alistair's body. "What happened?" she breathes. She studies the body more closely. "That's the man who rang the bell earlier."

Liam nods. "A small accident. He hit his head."

"Oh," Rosie says. It's clear she doesn't believe him. It's also clear she's not going to mention that. Instead, she says briskly, "I'll summon Horace, shall I? He'll get rid of him for you?"

Liam shakes his head. "I do need Horace. That other one you brought me didn't last long. I'll need him to get rid of it. It's in the usual room. Let's hope this one"— and here he nods once at the child— "is made of stronger stock." Then he returns to examining Alistair's body. "But this one . . . this one may be useful yet. He may be the key to this puzzle. This one may be quite . . . extraordinary." Then, he straightens up, pats Rosie on the cheek. "My girl," he says, his fingers lingering on the curve of her chin.

She smiles up at him, then says casually, "You know, Horace'll want the usual fee."

"He is mercenary, that one," Liam says with good humor. After crossing to his desk, he unlocks a side drawer. He fills Rosie's outstretched hand with what sounds like coins. The child's saucerlike eyes dart swiftly between Liam and Rosie, but otherwise he seems uncomprehending.

"Shall we move him, then?" Rosie says. Liam considers the body for a second, then nods. Kneeling down, he grasps Alistair's shoulders and heaves him across the floor. Rosie dances ahead of him to the wall opposite me, and pulls down a life-size portrait of a frowning woman dressed in white fur. Behind the painting is a small door, which she pushes open. Stepping aside, she watches as Liam heaves Alistair's body into the dark space beyond. Then she pulls the door shut.

"I'm going to wash up." Sighing again, he studies the spot where Alistair fell. "The carpet will have to be replaced," he says absently. "You summon Horace. Meet me back here at a quarter past eight. I have an appointment that I have to cancel."

"Do you need him, then?" she asks, jerking her thumb toward the child, who still doesn't seem to understand what's happening. "If you've already got—"

"Oh, no, no," Liam says fondly. "I can always use a spare. And besides, this one is different. Do you know he claimed to have a Talent?" He touches one finger to his lower lip as if anticipating the taste.

Rosie draws in a startled gasp. "But he . . . but then . . ."

Liam shrugs. "Of course, he's probably lying. But still, I have a few things I'd like to try."

Rosie turns her face up to his, reaches out one hand to his sleeve. "Will you let me . . . this time . . . will you let me try it, too?" She tugs harder at his arm. "You did promise. And if this one has the magic like he says, maybe it would work on me, too?" Her eyes flick toward the crystal goblet full of Alistair's blood.

Liam looks down at her, and something in his expression turns me even colder than I already am. "What an impatient, bloodthirsty little thing you are," he says, but his voice is detached, almost clinical. "When I think you're ready." As he turns away toward the door, a hungry look unravels across Rosie's face before her good-humored smile returns.

"I'll leave him here, then? The boy?"

Liam flaps his hand as he reaches the door. "Yes, yes. I'll be back shortly." And he leaves.

"You heard the master," Rosie says, her voice suddenly sugared over. "He'll see you in just a few moments."

The boy's eyes travel upward to her face. "And then you'll bring me the cake. Like you promised?" His tone is raggedly hopeful.

"Yes, just like I promised. Only you have to do everything the master says. Just like *you* promised." She gives the child a little shake until his head flops into a nod, and then she steps back, wiping her hands on her apron. "Now wait here and don't touch anything. Otherwise the master will know and he'll be very, very angry. And you don't want to see the master angry."

The child's gaze darts to the floor again and seems to hover on the blotch of Alistair's blood darkening the carpet. Seeming satisfied, Rosie slips after Liam.

As soon as the door closes, I scramble to my feet, and with splayed fingers, I grope along the passage, winding to my right. In just a few feet, the passage forks, one path leading to my right and one path leading downward to my left. I turn right and walk in what feels like a circle before the passageway widens again into an alcove. Although I'm fully expecting it, I still almost stumble over Alistair's body. For one long heartbeat, I freeze. I can't help it. Any second, I expect cold fingers to scrabble at my ankle. Then I crouch down by Alistair's body, studying his face in the meager light that spills through the eye-level grate.

His features are slack, almost as if he's wearing a rubber mask. Briefly, I wonder if this is what a dead person looks like before I force myself to put one hand on his chest. There is a faint, erratic beat beneath my fingers, much like the fluttering wings of a trapped bird. I pull my fingers back as if they've been singed.

And as if confirming my guess, Alistair's mouth suddenly twitches. A wet rattling hiss seems to be coming from his chest. "Tamsin Greene," he whispers, his lips cracking into a bloodstained smile. But his eyes remain closed.

I choke back my scream and wait in the shadows of the passageway for more. But after a minute, Alistair's breathing slows, then stills, and everything is silent. After a moment I realize I'm holding my own breath. *Please be dead, please, please.* And then I confront the horrible thought that if he isn't dead, I should kill him right now. I gather the folds of my skirts in my hands. If I pressed the material over his nose and mouth for long enough, I could end this all now. My family would be safe. I stare down the trickle of blood seeping from the back of his head, my fingers tightening my skirt into clumps of material.

I can't do it.

The thought of killing someone, even if it's Alistair, makes me dry heave.

With any luck he'll die here before Rosie gets back with Horace. Unable to even bring myself to touch his neck for a pulse, I step over his body, holding my skirts above my knees, and pull the door to the study open.

"Come with me," I say swiftly, but the child only stares at me. I try again. "You can't stay here. You're in horrible danger. Do you understand that?"

"She promised," he finally whines. "She promised me

meat and bread and all the cake I could eat." The word *cake* has a river of longing underneath it.

"She lied," I say brutally. "There's no cake. They're going to hurt you. Very badly. They're going to make you bleed." The child takes a step back, glances toward the door. Scrubbing his grimy hands together, he lifts them to his mouth. I study the torn and tattered shirt he's wearing, the cracked shoes that are a size too small judging from the way his big toes are poking out. "Come with me now and I'll get you cake. But you have to promise me something. Promise that you'll never come back here and that if you ever see that lady or that man again where you live, then you'll run as fast as you can the other way." I thought for a second and then added, "And you tell all the other children and their parents about these people."

"Don't have parents," the boy says at last. "None of us do." His fingers twitch at the hem of his shirt.

"Of course you don't," I mutter. "Okay, well, you tell all the other children you know never to go with this lady or this man. No matter what they promise." I wait until he nods and then I ask, "Have you seen them before?"

He nods again. "She came a while ago and went away with Sally. And then he came."

"The man here tonight?"

But the child shakes his head once. "'Nuther man. Small-like and . . ."

"Like a weasel or a rat?" I supply, and am rewarded with a half grin, revealing two missing bottom teeth.

"That's him. He took Jimmy." The child wipes his nose with a ragged bit of sleeve, then adds, "And Tommy."

It seems like Horace is quite the recruiter for the Knights. "You stay away from him, too, all right?"

"And you'll give me cake?" the boy asks, his eyes tip tilting upward.

Somehow I'll dig something out from the kitchen. I nod and just then hear a soft sound from outside the hallway.

"This way," I whisper, and shove the boy ahead of me. We scurry back into the passage.

"Is he dead?" the boy whispers as we skirt Alistair's body.

"I hope so," I say, then add, "Believe me, it would be a good thing." Grabbing his hand, I pull the child after me, praying I haven't made the biggest mistake of my life.

It feels like someone is squeezing my throat between iron fingers as we step out of the original doorway and back into the servants' landing. I half expect Rosie to be standing there with Liam, ready to smash me over the head. But no, the landing is empty except for the dusky shadows cast by the oil lamp. Putting my finger to my lips to warn the child, I pause for a few seconds, listening intently. But only the soft hiss of the wick burning reaches my ears, and so we start down the rest of the stairs as fast as I can make us go.

For once the kitchen is empty, too; I almost expected to see Cook snoring on top of the table. It never occurred to me to wonder where she sleeps, since she seems to be such a permanent fixture. *Cake, cake, where the hell would she keep the cake?*

As if reading my mind, the child steps out from behind me, his little nose twitching. "There," he says, pointing toward a large wooden breadbox. I rush over, push back the hatch, and find a batch of leftover scones, half a loaf of bread, and what looks like sugar cookies. Shaking open a cloth napkin, I dump all the contents of the breadbox inside and just manage to tie up the corners of the fabric. Then I swing the lumpy bundle toward him. His hands fasten over the cloth as if they'll never let go. Then his fingers start to fumble with the knot.

"Not here," I hiss. "Come on." I unlatch the door that leads to the back garden as quietly as I can. Still, it makes a horrible screeching noise that seems to rip apart the night's relative silence. I prod the child ahead of me and soon we come to the side gate that I entered only the day before with Horace. It seems more like ten years. I kneel down until I am eye level with the child and reach out to tousle his hair. Then I think better of it. "Now run away from here and don't look back, ever. And don't ever come back with that lady or with anyone else, okay?" Swallowing, I add, "And remember your promise to tell the other children."

With his eyes fixed on his precious bundle, he nods once. I shove him out the gate. He slips into the street and disappears like water down a crack in the sidewalk. Only then do I turn and creep back to the house, careful to keep out of sight of all the windows. But when I reach the kitchen door, I pause, then stretch my lungs in the deepest breath I can take. It's fresh air, even if it's soaked with the shadows of the Knight house.

There is a small stone bench running the length of the far wall, and after wandering over to it, I sink down on it. I tuck my stockinged feet up under me and wrap my arms around my knees and try to gulp in as much of the icy air as I can. I'm trembling and I don't think it's all from the cold.

I should have killed him when I had the chance. Was that my terrible choice? This question roars through my tired brain, followed by the thought that if Liam was even half right about my family, the Greenes of this century have no idea of what the Knights are up to. And it looks like the Knights are even worse than I imagined. And all I've managed to accomplish is to *not* kill Alistair when I had the chance. At least if I had done that, maybe history would get back on track and the Greenes would make the Domani and I could somehow help them to make it better so it would last.

The kitchen door creaks again and a backlit figure steps out of the house. I shrink farther into the shadows. Luckily, the moon has scudded behind the patchwork clouds. *Idiot, idiot, idiot.* It's probably Liam looking for the boy. Any second, Rosie will be back and somehow she'll know I had something to do with his escape.

But then the figure moves forward. It's Cook and she's walking slowly, stiffly, across the grass. At first I think she's asleep, but then the clouds drift apart like torn lace and the moon gilds her face, which is set and grim. Fascinated, I watch as she heads toward the statue of the woman that I first noticed when Horace brought me here.

Cook sniffles a little, the sound sharp in the otherwise silent garden. Then she lifts the hem of her apron and begins polishing the statue's face and hands. I frown. This seems to be taking housekeeping duties a little too seriously. Did La Spider demand that all her statues shine in the moonlight or something?

"I haven't forgotten you, Mary," she says, stroking the gray stone swirls of hair. "How could I? I'll find a way, I promise. If it's the last thing I do. I'll find a way to make them free you."

I lean forward, horror struck, hoping to hear more, but the side gate opens and Rosie and Horace step through. "And if he dies tonight, make sure that no one finds the body. The East River should do."

Horace nods once. Then he catches Rosie's hand and

starts kissing it. "Ah, my Rosie-Rose. When are you coming back to me? We had a good life, you and me. Didn't we? *Didn't we?*" It has suddenly become clear that Horace is not her uncle after all.

Rosie snorts. "Sure, we had a good life. When we had money. But now I don't have to worry about waking up cold or going hungry anymore. And he . . . he'll—"

Horace groans. "You can't think that he'll ever marry you, Rosie? You? A prostitute from Five Points?" And his groan turns into a wheezy sort of laugh.

"Control yourself," she says, stepping away from Horace. "He's promised me so much more than that. You'll see. And don't—" Rosie stops cold at the sight of Cook, who has straightened up, her apron clutched in her fists.

For one second they stare at each other. Then Rosie speaks first, in a taunting voice. "Still crying over that statue?" She circles her forefinger around her temple. "Get into the house, old woman, and get to bed, if you know what's good for you."

I force myself to remain still on my bench, reminding myself that it would do no good to leap up and turn Rosie herself into a statue.

Cook's face contorts as if she's about to spit at Rosie. But the girl pauses, one hand cocked on her hip, her elbow thrust forward at a sharp angle. Horace shuffles his feet, looking between the women. Finally, Cook's shoulders slump and she moves past Rosie toward the back door without a backward glance. Laughing, Rosie and Horace fall in after her. The kitchen door bangs once and they all disappear.

I stare at the statue again, at the woman's face frozen in a downward look as if she never saw what was coming for her. Then I tilt my head back and take in what stars I can in the heavy night sky. All at once, I can't bear it any longer. I close my eyes against the rush of longing for Gabriel that sweeps through me. It is so strong that when I open my eyes I half expect to see him standing in front of me.

But only moonlight and shadows chase through La Spider's immaculate garden, reminding me that I'm still alone.

FOURTEEN

"GET UP, AGATHA," ROSIE snaps. She sounds like she has been snapping for quite a while. Blearily, I peer at Rosie. She's standing over me, tapping her foot, neatly dressed as usual, every hair swept into place. But a scowl twists at her mouth, and I have to hide my answering grin. *Liam turned you out of his bedroom. Because the child got away and he's furious with you. Ha!*

Late last night, she had stomped back into our room, holding a candle. She hissed my name twice, and even though I was wide awake, I had mumbled something incomprehensible in my sleepiest voice and then rolled over toward the wall where I lay, listening to her huff around the room before finally settling into bed. Now I say in my sunniest voice, "Good morning, Rosie," and stretch my arms to the ceiling.

"None of that. Did you see anything last night or hear anything?" She watches my face intently as if determined to pry out the truth.

Dropping my arms, I stare at her. "See anything?" I pretend to think back. "No. I fell asleep early last night, being so tired and all. I did have the strangest dream about a swan and a rose and a beautiful horse. I think I was wearing a hat. Or maybe I wanted to wear a hat. No, actually, I was buying a hat— that was it! With pink roses on it."

I babble on and on, adding in random elements to my dream until Rosie turns away with a muttered, "You'd better get a move on or you'll get no breakfast again."

I leap out of bed.

In the kitchen, Cook is zipping around, barking orders at Dawn, who wields a rolling pin. Sparing me only a soft grunt, she indicates the tea tray with Jessica's morning cocoa. The kitchen clock says I have fifteen minutes, so I snatch a freshly baked roll from the rack on the counter when her back is turned and begin stuffing it in steaming pieces down my throat.

Which I promptly start to choke on when the door swings open and La Spider sweeps into the room. Thankfully, she doesn't even look at me. Instead, she is focused on Cook. And judging from the thin line of her lips, she's in a rage. A silence descends on the room like a shroud of fog and I force the lump of bread in my mouth to slide down my throat.

"I asked for oysters and turtle soup. Not *mussels*. And Mr. Tynsdell informs me that there won't be any crystallized fruits. Why?" La Spider touches the strand of pearls at her neck while eyeing the knives on Cook's cutting board. Suddenly, I know what it feels like to be a mouse with a cat in the room. I draw back farther into the corner. Behind La Spider, the door bumps open again and I see Rosie's unsuspecting face as she attempts to enter the kitchen. Without turning her head, La Spider crooks her little finger and the door slams shut, blotting out Rosie's startled look.

Cook's cheeks have turned the color of putty. But, twisting her apron in her hands, she faces La Spider and says, "I'm sorry, my lady. I did try. But they were out of the ones you like. I sent the girls to the market twice . . ." She makes a gesture toward Dawn, who opens her mouth, then promptly shuts it again.

"What a noble effort on your part," La Spider says dryly. Her eyes veer off toward the window as if observing something interesting out there. At the same time, Cook gives a sudden yelp of terror and her whole body slams back into the counter.

Again and again.

In the corner, Dawn covers her eyes while Lily sinks down, wrapping her arms around her knees. Tears begin to slide down her cheeks.

Cook grunts once and then seems to make an effort to not make any noise at all, as if knowing what La Spider requires.

Stop it. As easily as saying the words, I reach out and snap off La Spider's power. Slowly, La Spider turns her head and I feel her gaze search the room, probing the corners. I stare at my shoes, my hand squeezing the remaining half of the roll into crumbs, which trickle down my skirt. Cook is now making these little shuddery gasps.

"And what are you doing here?" La Spider says to me, her voice sharp enough to cut blocks of ice.

"Just coming to get Lady Jessica's cocoa, my lady," I say, waiting for the tingling that will pass over my skin if she decides to fling me across the room. My muscles tense in preparation of pretending to fall. But then her focus shifts back to Cook.

"I will expect the dishes I requested. All of them."

Cook's eyes fly open and she nods in stiff jerks. Her mouth opens to no doubt shape the words *Yes, my lady,* but La Spider speaks over her.

"Get back to work." And with that she exits the room, her shoe heels meeting the flagstone floor with quiet *chinks*.

"Get her some water," I say to Dawn as I hurry over to Cook, and then because Dawn doesn't move, I snap, "Now." This time she runs to fill a glass. "Can you move? Is anything broken?"

Cook shakes her head, but her face is still gray and she allows me to put my arm around her and lead her to the table. She is moving stiffly, but at least everything seems to be working.

"Jesus, Mary, and Joseph," Dawn is muttering over and over as she places the glass of water on the table. "Jesus, Mary, and Joseph."

"They won't come to this house," Cook whispers, then lifts the glass to her lips and drinks steadily. "I've prayed and prayed. But they won't come. Not to this house of sin." Water spills from her suddenly trembling mouth and slips down the side of her chin. I hand her a dishcloth, noticing only too late that it's covered with flour. But Cook only shakes her head and dabs her lips, leaving a smear of flour at the corner of her mouth. She looks at Dawn. "Go out and find the crystallized fruits. Try any market you can. And go to Delmonicos and buy whatever oysters they have. At any price."

"They'll be a fortune, Cook," Dawn gasps, but then scurries away as Cook tosses up her hands.

Sighing, Cook lowers her arms. "I'd like to poison the whole lot of them."

"Who?" I ask, sitting across the table from her.

"The Knight family. They're all coming to dinner tonight. And she makes me prepare the most elaborate meals. Ten courses. As if she's *the* Mrs. Astor. And still she won't hire any extra help. So when the stupid girl brings me back oysters and half of them aren't fit at all and I don't have time to find any more, well, you see what happens." She swipes at her eyes with the dishtowel and I resist the urge to reach over and brush away the flour that is now dusting her thick gray eyebrows. Then she gives me a slight smile. "You're a good girl, Agatha. Don't be like the rest of them. Don't go with Master Liam to his rooms at night."

I swallow. "I think Rosie's got that part of the job down."

Cook's mouth bunches up a little. "She gets jealous of any girl who looks twice at him. Why do you think they never last here? I've told Dawn and Lily time and again to keep their eyes down and their mouths shut. Thankfully, they do. And they look out for each other. But you—you should leave while you can."

"I'm working on it," I mutter.

Thirty-eight, thirty-nine, holy hell this is taking forever, forty-one, forty-two. While moving Jessica's ivory-handled brush through her hair, I've been counting out the strokes per Rosie's instructions. Fifty in the morning, one hundred at night before bed. Although it seems like no amount of brushing is going to transform Jessica's hair into anything from the heavy dull mat that it currently is.

"Enough," Jessica says at last. Gratefully, I put down the brush and pick up a handful of pins, just as La Spider makes her second appearance of the morning. My hand trembles. A pin falls to the floor.

In the mirror Jessica's face is set and tight, her smile brittle as she greets the older woman. "Mother. What a pleasant surprise. To what do I owe this honor?"

La Spider pauses in the doorway, takes in Jessica's

choice of gown this morning. "That color doesn't suit you at all," she says at last.

Secretly, I had thought the same thing earlier, but Jessica had insisted on the lime green morning dress and I wasn't about to argue with a Knight over clothes.

"Yes, it makes me look positively ghastly, doesn't it?" Jessica agrees, beaming at her mother as if the woman has just paid her the nicest compliment.

La Spider's hands twitch and I want to cry out to Jessica, *She's already chewed up and spit out one woman today.* Then I squelch down the feeling of loyalty to Jessica, feeling distinctly *un*loyal to my own family.

"Well, perhaps your new music tutor won't be so quick to fall in love with you as the last one was."

Jessica presses her hands together in her lap and takes a breath. "What do you mean, Mother?" she asks in a carefully blank voice that even I can tell is a dead giveaway.

So can La Spider, because she smiles from the doorway. "Just this morning, I've hired a new music tutor for you, since it seems you dismissed the last one. Did you think that your little shenanigan would go unnoticed?"

"My little shenanigan?" Jessica repeats carefully. Her eyes flicker to mine in the mirror. With the tiniest of motions, I shake my head. "I tired of the lessons. I'm not talented at all."

"Oh, I don't disagree with that. Nevertheless, a lady is expected to play at least three instruments—"

"Charmingly," Jessica finishes. "I know all that. Don't worry, Mother. I doubt that Edward Newcastle will refuse to marry me if I'm not able to dazzle him with my skills at the pianoforte. Your money and your title will be enough. Really, *you* should just marry him. Oh, I forgot—you're too old, aren't you? That would be *unseemly*."

I take a half step back, expecting Jessica or the furniture to go flying across the room. I steel myself to not stop it this time, because twice would be too coincidental. Besides which, I don't care if Jessica gets hurt. She's a Knight, after all. Not like Cook. Still, I find myself staring down at the eggshell-white part in her hair while fiercely willing La Spider to leave.

But La Spider only sighs. "How I ended up with you for a daughter is beyond me. Your new tutor is waiting for you in the drawing room. And then you and I will be lunching with the ladies' riding club. And then I believe you will have a caller this afternoon, so you will cancel all your engagements. You will listen to what Edward Newcastle has to say and you will be thrilled to accept his idea that the wedding will take place sooner than we planned. In fact, I will be giving a party to announce your engagement this weekend. Is that clear?"

"Yes, Mother. Thrilled," Jessica parrots, but she doesn't raise her eyes.

Her mother pauses, one jeweled white hand on the

doorknob. "And if you misbehave or cross me in any way this afternoon, if there is anything other than the result I expect, then understand that your Mr. Finnegan will pay for it. Dearly."

Jessica dips her chin in what her mother must take for a nod. La Spider delivers her parting shot while exiting. "Change that dress. Now. And burn it."

FIFTEEN

"WELL, FIND ANOTHER GUTTER brat, then! I'm counting on this little piece of entertainment for tonight."

Halfway across the foyer, I freeze. La Spider's tones ring across the hallway, and even as I look around for a place to hide, I wonder if it's even necessary. She doesn't seem to care what her servants know about her. Or rather, she doesn't seem to even realize that her servants have any brains to process anything at all. So I creep closer to the door that leads to her study and, after a second, press my ear to the wooden panel.

"Horace is looking right now and Rosie was supposed to—" Liam's voice chokes off with a wet gargle. "Mother," he gasps finally. "I'm rather fond of my windpipe."

"Horace! I never want to see that toad of a man. And you put too much stock in that girl. Don't think I don't know what's going on between you two."

"She's useful to me, Mother. That's all."

"They're all useful. Up to a point. But to consort with a human like that? *Filthy.*" The violence in that last word makes me take a step back.

"Will there be anything else?" Liam asks finally, his voice dipped in frost to match his mother's tone.

"Not for now. Use Jessica's maid if you have to, but no more after that. People will start to talk if we lose another maid," La Spider answers. The sound of footsteps makes me scamper across the marble foyer. The door swings open and Liam strides out. His eyebrows jut together across his face; his mouth is caught in mid-snarl. He looks like a lion awakened at just the wrong moment. I flatten myself next to a large gilt-edged mirror, but he catches sight of me, stops suddenly.

"Agatha," he purrs pleasantly, and like smoke in the wind, all traces of anger wisp off his face. He advances on me. "And how are you finding our pleasant household?"

A minefield.

But I give him a quick, appropriately shy smile back and even bob a half curtsy. "Very well, sir. It suits me fine."

His smile broadens. "Wonderful. And how is my sister? Not too strict a taskmistress, I hope?"

"Oh, no, sir. Lady Jessica is lovely. Truly lovely."

Liam's eyebrow shoots up as if he can't help himself before he leans closer. The smell of his aftershave, spicy sweet, begins to prick at my nose. I shift my arms and try to step forward, but he's caged me in too effectively. "You can tell me if she works you too hard. Makes you run around too much. Mending this, mending that." He gives a wave of his hand.

I flick my own eyebrow upward. "Truly, sir. She's fine."

"Good, good," he says, and begins to turn away. But I don't let myself take a deep breath yet. "You know," he begins, and looms back over me. "I wonder if you might help me out with something, then." His voice slips into a murmur. "If my sister can spare you."

I swear he almost salivates over the word *spare*.

"I'm sure whatever you need help with Mr. Tynsdell can do for you. I don't know much about cravats or suits or bowler hats."

"Oh, no, no, no," Liam says, and now he's smiling down at me. The muscles in his shoulders flex under his thin white shirt as he leans up against the wall. With the lightest touch, he traces the curve of my cheekbone.

Poor Livie and the other girls. He treated them the same way. And I can only imagine how they went all fluttery and did exactly what he wanted. *Wrong girl*, I want to snap at him. Just as I'm about to slam my palm into his forehead and test out whether or not Aunt Beatrice's Talent has deserted me, he says, "I need you. Just for something small," he coaxes, and all at once a tingling radiates across my nerves. The edges of Liam's outlines start to quiver and ripple.

Bracing my boots on the floor, I look up at him, making sure to keep a slightly glazed-over expression on my face. "Sir," I whisper, making sure to put just enough of a tremble into my voice. "I . . . I feel so dizzy."

Actually, I feel just the opposite. Really, maybe I should major in drama when I get to college.

Liam draws back suddenly, confusion scrolling across his face. I lower my lids and let my lips tremble as I lean into him. "I felt so strange for a moment there."

Come on, you sick bastard. One more time and then we'll see how you like it when someone jumps inside of you.

"Oh," I cry, letting one hand flutter up to my chest. "Sir, I—"

"Agatha," says a sharp voice, cutting through my act. Liam steps backwards and now I really do stumble a little. Rosie's cheeks are brick red, as if she's just been slapped, and her hands are twisted together. But her voice evens out as she says, "You're late with Lady Jessica's tea in the music room."

I cast a sidelong glance at Liam, whose face has smoothed over. He nods at me as if we've just encountered each other in the foyer. As I slip past Rosie toward the kitchen, the look of loathing she gives me sizzles into the side of my face.

But I can't keep from smiling once I'm out of both of their sights. All I need is to get Liam to use his Talent one more time against me.

❧

Brisk piano playing streams forth from the music room, so I don't bother to knock. Not that I could have anyway, since my hands are full with balancing the tea tray.

Jessica is seated at the piano, her hands moving across the keys while her new tutor is turning the pages on the music stand. I barely look at them as I cross the room and set the tray down on the small side table. Hidden from view, I begin pouring the tea into the porcelain cups. Obviously, Liam managed to extract poor Livie's blood by slipping into her body—she probably had no memory of what happened to her each time. He must have bled her and let her stumble back to her duties not understanding why she was growing weaker and weaker.

The piano music crescendos and then fades away. "I'll take the tea over here, Agatha," Jessica says. I nod, arranging the lumps of sugar with the silver tongs on a small saucer. Hooking the cups with my fingers, I start across the room toward Jessica and her new music tutor, who finally raises his face from the music stand and meets my eyes directly.

Hot tea scalds my fingers as the cup falls to the carpet.

It's Gabriel.

"Agatha!" Jessica's voice rings out, sharp with reproof, a thin echo of her mother's.

"I'm so sorry, my lady," I murmur, and rescue the cup

from the floor. Black tea leaves dot the backs of my fingers. "I'll get a fresh cup. It won't happen again."

"See that it doesn't," Jessica says. I bite down hard on my lip and rush out the door.

Of course this is what would happen. You wanted him to come and now he's here and now he's going to be in danger and it's all your fault. Liam will get to him somehow and learn how to Travel. Stupidstupidstupid.

I dash into the kitchen, ignoring Cook's surprised look, snatch a fresh cup from the shelf, and dash back out.

Back in the music room, Gabriel is holding up the music book again and turning the pages. "I think your left hand needs strengthening. I noticed it on that last piece. I don't want you to attempt this piece again until you've mastered this one here and here," he says, indicating the pages. My heart can't help but float upward at the sound of his voice, the first truly friendly one I've heard in days.

Jessica's eyes move rapidly and she nods, seeming casually interested. She gives me a sidelong look but doesn't comment as I rush over to the tray and begin pouring a second cup. I've got time to observe that Gabriel seems to be dressed in exactly the perfect 1880s apparel. Freshly pressed dark trousers and a matching vest with a gleaming white shirt underneath. His hair's been tied back. No patches or dust or the overwhelming scent of mothballs, which means he didn't find his new clothes in my family's attic.

"Sugar in your tea? Sir?" I ask as I hand Jessica her first cup.

His eyes meet mine again. "Thanks, but I'm not in a sugary mood today, *Agatha*."

Okay. This is not going to go well.

Jessica gives him a puzzled glance over the rim of her cup, but I nod and return to my tray, feeling the back of my neck burn. I fuss as long as I can over the cup, listening as Gabriel gives Jessica more instructions. Finally, after handing him his cup, which he accepts without even looking at me, I ask Jessica if she needs anything else. She shakes her head, dismissing me.

"I'll just be close by. Very close by, if you need anything, my lady," I state loudly, and she flashes me an annoyed glance before turning back to the music book.

Heading to the door, I do my best not to look back, because then I'll want to do something undeniably stupid like fling myself into Gabriel's arms.

SIXTEEN

I SLIP INTO THE NEXT ROOM after a cautious knock to make sure that it's empty. It seems to be yet another parlor where the family could receive guests. Who knew you needed so many of these places?

I pace three times around a pink love seat and a matching pink chair, and then change directions before stopping to watch the squares of morning sunlight inch across the floral rug. Finally, the door opens.

"What are you doing here?" I hiss as soon as Gabriel shuts the door behind him. Okay, that wasn't the first thing I meant to say. Or even the second. It's just what came out.

"Looking for you, you idiot," he hisses back, and takes four strides toward me.

"You can't be here," I say desperately. "You don't understand. Liam is going to—"

But now he's reached me. As he pulls me into his arms, I lift my face to his. "Oh, no," he states. "Don't even think we're about to kiss and make up. You. Are. In. So Much. Trouble." He punctuates each statement with a shake.

"Ouch! Stop. What are you talking about? In trouble with you? Why?"

Gabriel stops shaking me but doesn't let go of my upper arms. Instead, he regards me evenly in silence. "Tamsin," he says. I almost want to cry with the relief of having someone use my real name. "You're a smart girl. But let me walk you through this. Now think. Why would I—"

"All right, all right. I get it. Because I've been blocking you from finding me."

"Not just that," Gabriel interjects.

"Okay, I didn't tell you I was leaving. But that's only because I didn't want you to come with me. It's too dangerous. You don't—"

Gabriel's eyes narrow and I swallow hard before pressing on. "Okay, maybe you don't like hearing that, but it's the truth."

"It's too dangerous for me, but not for you?" he asks softly. Meanwhile, his fingers have tightened on my shoulders again.

"Okay, seriously, I know that the male ego probably can't handle hearing that, but—"

"You don't get to make my decisions for me, Tamsin. Is that clear? I would think that of all people you would understand just how frustrating that is." Abruptly, he drops his hands from my shoulders and steps away from me.

The distance yawns between us.

Blurry gold bars of sunlight slide across the floor. I blink until I can see clearly again. "I'm sorry," I whisper finally.

Gabriel nods. "You should have told me," he says in a low, colorless voice. "You should have told me what you were planning to do. And when Rowena told me what happened, I couldn't even find you anyway . . ." He twists his vest as if it's suddenly choking him. "I thought you . . . I thought you had died," he adds flatly.

I take a step forward. "Gabriel—"

"But then I realized that no, I would have been able to at least find your body. So I kept trying. And then I realized you were blocking me."

A pulse is twitching in the skin over his throat, and I want to touch him but realize that's probably not a good idea right now. Instead, I say, "I stopped. Last night, I thought about it and I knew that it . . . that I really wanted you . . ." My voice trails off. Apparently that was the wrong thing to say, too. Instead of leaping all over that statement and making one of his usual innuendos, Gabriel gives me that same hard look that means he's still angry.

"I didn't just arrive last night," Gabriel says.

I try not to let my jaw drop. It does anyway. "You didn't? But I was . . . when did you get here, then?"

"Yesterday morning." He pauses, then adds, "I'm actually not at your beck and call, Tamsin."

"I didn't say you were," I say, my cheeks suddenly burning. "I . . . okay, how did you arrive, then?"

"You weren't blocking me from Traveling. You were blocking me from finding you. So, I looked for Alistair. Easy enough."

"Oh." I shut my mouth with a snap. There doesn't seem to be anything to add to that.

"What?" Gabriel asks.

"Nothing," I snap. "It's just . . . I'm annoyed that I didn't think of that." I study the vines running through the square of wool carpet at my feet.

"You're *annoyed*? You're annoyed that I'm smarter than you?"

"You're not *smarter* than me," I blaze, looking up at him. And sure enough, he's laughing at me. "How dare you! How dare you laugh at me!"

"Wow, you're even starting to talk like you're from the 1800s. Are you going to stamp your foot now and toss your head at me?" And he starts laughing even harder.

"No," I mutter, but I'm trying not to smile now. "Jerk."

"And may I say you look pretty damn hot in that maid's uniform. How come you never dress up like that for me?"

I roll my eyes. "I take it you've forgiven me."

"You take it wrong," Gabriel says lightly, and then closes the distance between us again. "But you can try to persuade me to."

I lean back in his arms, tilt my face up to him again, and flutter my eyelashes in an exaggerated manner. "I thought you said we're weren't going to kiss and make up."

"That was then, Tam, this is now. Now shut up."

And then he's kissing me like crazy. I wrap my arms around his neck, my nails digging into his shoulders. I decide to let myself forget all about the Knights for a moment. Or two.

Approximately fifteen minutes later, during which we've stumbled our way over to a pink love seat and I've lost most of my hairpins, Gabriel lifts his head and says suddenly, "By the way, I found your family."

"What?" I ask in a dazed voice.

"Your family in this century. I found them. They're—"

I struggle to sit up. "Just *now* you found them? Right now? I'm sort of offended that you—"

Gabriel grins down at me. "Not *now*, now. When I came here. I figured you'd need my help sooner or later."

Searching for hairpins in the couch, I say, "If you weren't so cute, I'd find you really annoying." Finally, I find one, jam it into my hair, and stand up. "Are you ready? Let's get the hell out of here."

Gabriel arches an eyebrow at me. "What, and lose your job? Have you even been paid yet?"

I snort. "I'm so done with being a lady's maid."

I don't think I breathe once until Gabriel and I have safely slipped out the side gate. Then, holding hands, we break into a run down Twenty-seventh Street, dodging carriages, pedestrians, and carts full of produce. The wind whips at my ankles and slips under the hem of my dress. It feels delicious.

"We could be back in New York tonight. I mean *our* New York," I say as we sidestep a group of well-dressed boys. They are playing some sort of complicated-looking game that involves tossing marbles into a circle drawn on the cobblestones.

"Yeah," Gabriel says, his eyes scanning the street. "It is kind of amazing here, though. I mean, how many people can say they saw Old New York in—"

"Don't even think it," I say, and press my fingers over his mouth for good measure. "You remember what I told you about the effects of Traveling."

Gabriel kisses my fingers. "We've got a long trip ahead of us. Your family's uptown. And I mean *way* uptown. In fact, I don't think we can call it town. It's more farmland."

"Pig farmers," I say slowly, remembering Liam's derisive laughter.

"Excuse me?" Gabriel says.

I nod. "Yep, pig farmers. There's a lot I've got to fill you in on," I say as Gabriel waves down a hansom cab drawn by two black horses. The one closest to me tosses its head as the driver pulls the carriage to a stop.

I raise one eyebrow at Gabriel. "Wow. And here I thought we'd take the elevated train."

"It doesn't go up that far. Besides, Tam," Gabriel adds, "you've always wanted me to take you for a carriage ride in Central Park."

"No, I haven't."

"Oh, really," Gabriel says absently, as the driver clambers down from his perch and whisks out a folding step. "That must have been some other girl, then."

"What?" I punch him in the arm. Our driver blinks, then looks away quickly.

"Appearances, Tam," Gabriel says out of the side of his mouth as he practically shoves me into the carriage. "We're in the nineteenth century, after all."

"Was that Central Park West back there?" I ask. Our driver touches his cap once, then shakes the reins and the horses move off down the lane. The carriage couldn't make it any farther down the dirt path that Gabriel had directed our driver to.

Even though I've been in the 1800s for days now, every once in a while I still expect the New York City I know, full of skyscraper buildings and yellow taxis and limos and skateboarders, to superimpose itself on all this. I take a deep breath. It's quieter. The reach and sprawl of the city seems to lose its grasp here. A while ago we had passed what looked like a stately apartment building and I had read the sign in a blur: THE DAKOTA. But farther north here, the country is still undeveloped and wild-looking—a tangle of trees and brush and winding dirt paths and parkland and farmhouses. Prosperous farmhouses, though.

"That's the one," Gabriel says softly, nodding toward the closest of the white stone buildings. In the muted light, the stones seem to glow, the windows sparkle, and the pigs, if my family happen to be pig farmers, seem to be contained neatly in some invisible pen. A white windmill churns slowly, and smoke dribbles out from one of the several brick chimneys, a fluted gray column that thins and dissolves into the sky. Blackbirds, too many of them to count, are perched on one gable, eyeing us relentlessly. I would think they're carved from obsidian until one of them flicks a wing open and resettles it. A breeze touches down on an iron weathervane in the shape of a prancing horse, making it spin faster and faster.

"They know we're here," I say suddenly, staring at the windows. The sun, emerging from behind a shawl of clouds, winks and gleams on the diamond panes, sending edges of light dancing across the stone walls.

"Then let's go introduce ourselves," Gabriel says, and folds his hand over mine.

SEVENTEEN

THE FRONT GATE IS UNLOCKED and swings
open on well-oiled hinges. Still, the coven of birds on the
roof takes flight in one wheeling mass. No one seems to
be around in the late afternoon, but we both approach the
massive front door cautiously, almost on tiptoe. And then,
like a dream image, a large silver dog appears from the corner of the farthest outbuilding. It sights us, tips its ears up,
and moves toward us on silent paws.

Huge paws. To go with its huge teeth on display in its
open mouth.

"Um . . . think that's their attack dog?"

"That's not a dog," Gabriel says, his hand tightening
on mine. "That's a wolf."

I blink. I've only seen pictures of wolves, but now
that he mentions it, there's something definitely "not dog"
enough about this animal. Maybe it's the complete lack of
recognition in its eyes of us as anything other than meat.
Maybe it's the way its legs are bent at sharp angles, clearly

built for massive speed. Or maybe it's the way its jaws are designed for crushing larger animals between its teeth.

I reach out silently, praying that this is one of my family members in disguise. Nothing. The wolf stalks forward, tufts of silver-gray fur spiking up in clumps along its spine. Definitely not a good sign in animal-speak.

"Okay," I say as the wolf closes the gap between us to fifteen feet, then ten. "Let's hope Aunt Beatrice's Talent hasn't decided to desert me."

"That's a plan," Gabriel says, edging in front of me.

I throw a glance at the door and note the griffin-shaped door knocker. I reach out for the brass ring enclosed in its talons.

The griffin's wings ripple and its beak moves. "Friend or foe?" it intones.

"Friend. Family," I add quickly. Who would identify themselves as a foe anyway? Especially with a wolf heading toward them?

The griffin's beak clicks shut as if seeming to consider this. "Please hurry," I urge it.

It turns its head and regards me with its carved brass eye. It considers some more.

Just then the wolf reaches Gabriel and me. The sharp animal smell rising from its fur washes over me. Its tongue slides from the side of its open mouth. Three drops of saliva fall to the stone walkway. It looks hungry.

Then it turns its head sharply as if called by its master.

A girl emerges from the same direction as the wolf. She is carrying a wide wicker basket filled with all kinds of plants and roots, some of which fall to the ground as she catches sight of us.

"It's the crow girl," I whisper to Gabriel. "The one I told you about."

"Seems like she's a wolf girl, too," he whispers back, his eyes still fastened on the wolf, who is now sniffing around our legs with pointed concentration.

"Hello again," I say weakly. "Sorry for yesterday. When I made you fall. I know you said you'd find me, but—"

"You found me first," she says, but there is no surprise in her voice.

Sunlight splashes down on the walkway, shining across her bare feet, which are covered in dirt. Leaves have tangled themselves in her waist-long red hair, and a muddy streak covers one forearm. More mud dots the front of her skirt. Despite her unkempt appearance, she is every bit as beautiful as the last time I saw her.

For a long moment, she seems to be deciding what to say next, but then finally settles on "Silvius warned me there were strangers on the path," the girl says as she approaches us.

"That's good," I manage, feeling the heat of the animal's breath through my thin skirt. "Is Silvius your wolf?"

At that she laughs, her eyes scrunching up into half moons of delight. "Not *my* wolf. Silvius is nobody's wolf," she adds, scrubbing the animal's head with her knuckles. But Silvius's actions seem to disagree with that as he bumps up against her hip with his long snout, then licks her hand with that pink tongue. "And the birds also," she says distantly, her eyes scanning the sky. "The birds."

Gabriel and I exchange glances. "We—"

"You'd better come in, then. Thom's been waiting for you for a while."

"Oh," I say, and close my mouth. Hopefully this is going to be easier than I expected. But her next words drive that hope right out of my head.

"Although not everyone agrees that you're what you seem. Not everyone wants you to come here."

She taps the griffin's beak once, then waits while it fluffs its wings and resettles its head under them. This seems to be the signal for her to push open the door. We follow her. The floors are a wide-planked honey-colored wood and the furniture is solid and heavy and plain, but clearly good quality. Logs are stacked in abundance at one edge of the fireplace guarded by two china dogs that look very familiar. The last time I saw them they were spilling everything to Rowena in my family's library.

Three people are seated on a long low couch adjacent to the fire. The girl leads us to them, then stops and gestures us forward. I can't help but get the feeling that we're standing before a panel of judges. A woman who could be anywhere from forty to sixty is seated between two men.

Her eyes probe mine, then skip over to Gabriel, then back to me. I wait for the tingle to slip over my skin, indicating that she's attempting to use her Talent on me, but nothing happens. One of the two men turns his head and whispers something to her, but she raises her hand in a little motion and he falls silent.

Okay, so it's clear who's in charge here. I study the woman more closely as the girl says, "I found them on the path."

The woman nods. "Thank you, Isobel."

The girl shrugs, then adds, "Silvius vouches for them."

A flicker of annoyance crosses the woman's face, but the man brings his hand to his mouth to suppress a cough that sounds a little too much like laughter. "Thank you, Isobel," the woman says again, but this time it sounds more like "Goodbye, Isobel."

Turning swiftly, Isobel heads toward the door with the wolf padding close behind her. Then the second of the two men leans forward, his face no longer in shadow, and I gasp. "You!"

Gabriel tightens his hand on mine, so I know he recognizes him, too. But there is no recognition in this man's eyes. "It hasn't happened yet," Gabriel breathes next to me, and I nod slightly. Still, that's hard to make myself realize, since the last time I saw this man, he was doing his best to kill us.

"I beg your pardon," he says in that cultured voice that I remember all too well. I close my eyes briefly. *You really don't know what you've done, do you?*

Now I shake my head. "Sorry—the last time I saw you, you tried to set us on fire."

Seeing the confusion on his face, I backtrack. "It hasn't happened yet. It happens in 1899. But no hard feelings. You didn't succeed," I say, realizing a little too late how bad this sounds.

And just in case I needed more confirmation, Gabriel mutters, "Smooth, Tam."

The man's frown deepens and then he exchanges glances with the woman. "Thom made no mention of that incident. Why?"

The woman shakes her head. "Perhaps because he didn't foresee it. Or because it doesn't happen."

"So they're lying," the man adds, his voice crisply decisive, and I feel prickles of annoyance at that smug, familiar tone. He sounded exactly the same in 1899, right after he nearly burned Gabriel's hand off.

"No, we're not lying," I snap, too impatient to wait any longer. "I don't know who Thom is, but I'm guessing he's the one who reads the book in your time?"

Silence as three pairs of eyes regard me.

"You know the book I'm talking about," I say impatiently. Out of the corner of my eye, I see Gabriel give a warning shake of his head, but I ignore it. "Then you'll also know who I am and why I've come here."

The woman leans forward, studying me again, before she speaks. "All we know is what Thom can see—which is that a stranger came to town and entered the house of the Knights."

"That's Alistair," I cry out.

But she continues as if I haven't spoken. "She is a harbinger of death."

"Wait . . . what?"

"She's not," Gabriel says hotly, having apparently decided to abandon the calm and collected routine.

"I'm not a harbinger of death," I say at the same time. I thought I was supposed to be a beacon. According to my grandmother.

But the woman is shaking her head. "If we listen to you, we face peril and a change in our way of life. A change so great that we cannot ever return to what we were before. That's what the book tells us."

"Then your Thom isn't very skilled at reading it," I say, wishing that this Thom had one-tenth of the foresight of my grandmother.

"Thank you," a voice says from behind me, and I jump.

A third man crosses the room, leaning heavily on a cane. Halfway between us and the couch, he stops and flicks his hand toward an unlit lamp on a side table. It flares to life, illuminating his long, craggy nose and chin. "That's not all it says, you know," he adds in a mild tone as he settles himself into an armchair adjacent to the couch.

The three people on the couch turn to him, but it's the woman who speaks. "What else did you see?" she whispers, as if she doesn't want to know. She puts one hand to her curly hair, and my throat suddenly aches. The gesture reminds me of my mother.

The man leans forward a little and regards me curiously. "Apparently, you aren't just the harbinger of death. You're the harbinger of my death." He nods, as if impressed with whatever it is I'll do to bring this about, before pulling out his handkerchief again.

I stare at the man again, then at his cane. It's the same person I saw on the street corner at dusk. "You were standing on the street. The other day at the Knights' house. You made the lights go out."

He smiles at me just as the woman on the couch gasps softly. "Thom," she says. "You didn't tell me this. Why would you go there?"

Now the man shrugs, examines a button on his overcoat as if it's fascinating. "If you knew who was going to kill you, wouldn't you be curious to catch a glimpse of him or her?"

This is too much for me and apparently for the woman on the couch.

"I'm not going to kill you," I snap just as the woman says, "This is just further proof that we *cannot* have anything to do with her, Thom." Then she turns to me, takes a deep breath, and says, "You must leave at once and not come back here."

"Ignoring the future won't make it go away, Cera," Thom says, and now he smiles at her. There's a bittersweet tone to his voice. "And death comes for us all. This young person seems like a rather charming vehicle, when you think about it."

"Enough," says the third man, the one who hadn't spoken yet. "Cera has decided, and Thom, based on what you revealed, it seems wise of her to caution this. Unless you're not revealing everything?"

Thom sighs, presses two fingers to the bridge of his nose in a gesture that my grandmother will learn in another century. It makes me wonder if reading the family book brings on blinding headaches or something. "Nothing is ever revealed completely. All I know is, this young woman and young man," he adds with a nod to Gabriel, "have Traveled a long way to warn us, and whether we listen or not, the future is uncertain. They don't mean us harm, but this young woman will be the harbinger of—"

"The Knights are killing people," I burst out. Everyone turns back to me. There is a silence like a collective breath being held. "By taking too much of their blood. At least one servant girl I know has died, probably more. And their blood is making the Knights stronger." And then, because still no one speaks, I add, "They're *killing* people."

"We know that," the man from 1899 says. Those three flat words shock me into silence.

"We *suspected* that," Cera corrects. "They've always been . . . fond of experimenting on humans."

Behind my back, I flex the fingers of my right hand wide, then dig them into the palm of my left hand, all while staring at her. "So you don't care? Because they're only humans? *What are you?*"

She recoils from my tone, her head moving sharply until I am left with her profile as she exchanges glances with the two men on the couch. "Years ago, La Spider came to our mother." She gestures toward the two men sitting on either side of her. "I was not much older than Isobel, and I remember listening at the doorway as she proposed that we join them in expanding their power. La Spider told my mother that we placed too much emphasis on the four elements while ignoring the fifth."

"The fifth?" I ask.

Cera's lips tighten with distaste. "Blood. If only we would explore its properties. She enumerated all the possibilities of what we could do with this unlimited power at our grasp." Cera puts one hand to her throat as if to swallow the memory. "Fortunately, our mother declined. She explained to La Spider that we have always been a quiet people, choosing to live here, where there are not many to observe us, to comment on our way of life." She sighs.

"That's all changing now," Thom says gently, as if reminding her of another discussion.

She doesn't look at him, but nods, her face folding downward. "La Spider called my mother a fool, a child content to play in her gardens. But she left. More important, *she left us alone.* And we've lived in peace ever since."

"Do you understand that the more you ignore them, the worse off you'll be?" Gabriel says suddenly, taking a step forward. "Do you know what happens in a hundred years? You defeat them now, but they rise again and then all of your lives are threatened."

"More than threatened. There will be no Greenes left. That's what our book says in our time," I add.

"But time is so unpredictable, and clearly if we defeat them as you say, then they'll rise to seek revenge." She pauses, then continues, her voice inflexible. "Perhaps it's something we never should have involved ourselves with in the first place."

I want to scream. Of all the possibilities, I never envisioned this. Then I stop and think about that. Why *didn't* I envision this? I know the ugly underside of how my family feels about people who aren't Talented. I've lived through it myself. Taking a steadying breath, I put one hand on Gabriel's arm, then say, "What if it's not just humans they're experimenting with? What if they move on to experimenting on one of you?"

Cera's eyes widen. The man from 1899 makes a polite noise in his throat that conveys disbelief, while his brother shakes his head. Only Thom remains still, his gaze anchored on mine. Finally, Cera says to Thom, "Have you seen this? Tell the truth!"

He rubs the bridge of his nose again, sighs, and finally says, "Not yet."

"It won't happen," Cera says. "La Spider and her brood may be bloodthirsty, but they're not fools. For better or for worse, we've agreed to exist with each other's perceived . . . shortcomings." Her words are crisp and decisive.

"But it does happen," I say frantically. "Even if Thom here can't see it at the moment. They—"

"Then there is no need to act rashly. What you say may never come to pass." She stands abruptly, and all three men come to their feet, Thom last of all, as he struggles with his cane.

"Please," I beg him, searching his face for some spark of understanding. "People are dying. Children. Girls. You have to do something about it. You can't just . . . You must see what is going to happen."

He sighs and seems about to answer me, but before he can, Cera steps in front of him. Folding her hands together as if offering a benediction or a blessing, she says, "Thank you, Tamsin, for coming here. You've Traveled a long way, and we do appreciate your efforts. But it's best if you return to your own time now, as you should know that Traveling is forbidden. We'll consider your warning carefully with all due weight."

Translation: *Go away now and we'll agree to forget that you ever came here.*

EIGHTEEN

GABRIEL AND I ARE SILENT as we walk back down the path. The sky has turned to white-gray and the breeze is now edged with the scent of rain.

"That went well," Gabriel says, his voice bleak.

"What did we do wrong? Why won't they believe us? Why are they so *stupid?*"

"They're afraid," Gabriel says slowly. "They're afraid of you. Afraid to act. Afraid to—"

"Why?"

"It happens all the time, Tam."

I look up at him.

"History," he offers. "You see it all the time in history."

I'm not really in the mood for a history lesson, but Gabriel continues.

"People don't want to believe the worst can happen until it's happening and it's—"

"Too late," I finish grimly.

Slowly, we begin walking back in the direction of the city. Trees tower overhead, lining the path, blocking out the sunlight.

After we've walked in silence for at least a mile, and after the blister on my right foot has turned into a knot of pain, I say, "They don't care. You heard them. It's just humans the Knights are killing. *It doesn't concern us*," I mimic Cera's voice. "How could she? How could any of them act like that when—how could they know this is happening and still let it happen?" I squeeze my eyes shut, but still I can't shut out the memory of Alistair's voice in his office at NYU. *Is that what you think? That we were murdering people and therefore the Greene family swooped in and saved the day? Lies. Your family cared nothing, nothing about who we took for ourselves as long as it wasn't one of their own.*

A wagon splatters past us, sending up a sheet of mud. Gabriel pulls me to the side just in time to avoid adding a whole new layer of dirt to my clothes.

"We should've tried to hitch a ride on that one," he remarks. We walk in silence for another few minutes before he says, "I don't know that they don't care. After all, we know that eventually the Greenes do rise up and defeat the Knights."

The stately apartment building has come back into view. As I stare at it, something unfurls in my mind. I stop walking. "They don't care about humans. But they did start caring really fast when the Knights moved on to experimenting on them. Somehow, the Knights must have gotten one of the Greenes. But that's not going to happen now, is it? Or at least not yet."

"Why not?" Gabriel asks.

"Thom's not seeing that they're going to experiment on the Greenes because they don't need to yet. Now that they have Alistair. They'll learn how to take someone's Talent, and then it'll be too late for the Greenes to resist. Plus, they'll know that the Greenes are going to try to make the Domani because Alistair already told them, I'm sure. The clock," I gasp. "We need to steal that clock and bring it to the Greenes before it's too late. Do you—?" I break off my words to study Gabriel's face. "What? What aren't you telling me?"

He opens his mouth, then looks away from me, apparently focused on a bedraggled group of children as they run through the street, chasing one small boy ahead of them. A soft rain begins to fall. "I can't find anyone right now," he says at last, still not looking at me.

"What?" Now it's my turn to grab his chin and pull it toward me so he has to meet my eyes. "Who?"

"I can't find anyone from your family. Your mom, your sister, your grandmother. I can't even find my mother. I can find my dad."

"Well, that's something," I mutter, but we're both too worried to smile. Gabriel's dad, Phil, is what the rest of my family, past and present, would call a mere human. He's Talentless.

"But it's like the rest of your family and even mine doesn't exist."

I sigh, lean against Gabriel's shoulder, watching a hansom carriage roll past, the horses' heads hanging low. "Okay, so." I hold up the fingers of my left hand and begin folding them down with each pronouncement. "We found my family. They don't currently believe us. Now we'll just have to handle this ourselves."

"They'll have to believe us. At some point."

I nod, scan Gabriel's face anxiously. Raindrops glitter on his cheekbones and fuse his dark eyelashes into spikes. There's a slight flush under his skin. How much time does he have before . . . ? But I can't even finish that thought, so I shake my head and instead say, "Great. Okay. We need to fix this right away. We can't go back home; we can't stay here forever." I'm glad my voice is so steady, because a cold trembling is welling up somewhere from deep inside of me. "Why don't I just go back to the Knights' house and steal the clock, then we head back to my family's doorstep and camp out there until someone else dies and they decide to believe us?"

"That sounds like such a good plan," Gabriel says with a snort.

"So, you've got a better one?"

"Yeah," he says, shielding me from another mud-splattering carriage. "One that involves you not going back to the Knights' house."

"I'm listening."

There's a pause as he scans the gray sky. "Yeah, I'm still working out the rest of it. I only got that part down. The part about you never going near the Knights again."

Digging one foot into the cobblestones, I point out, "Actually, you're in way more danger than I am."

"Explain that?"

I roll my eyes. "Besides the obvious? At some point in time, Liam gets you. That's how he was able to Travel to the future."

Gabriel sighs. "We don't know that for sure. It may not happen—"

"Now you sound like my family," I say.

"Okay, okay. Let's steal the clock tonight. Both of us. We'll head back—"

"Tonight they're having some kind of dinner," I say slowly. "I think all the Knights are coming. So I could go back, pretend I had to visit some dying aunt or something if they ask where I was, and then I'll let you in the side gate at eight? They should all be at dinner, so they'll be occupied. We should be okay."

Gabriel sighs. "I don't like it."

"What else is new?"

"I mean it, Tam. Too many things could go wrong."

"Which is why it'd be safer if I just did it by myself and you—"

But he's glaring at me now.

I hold up my hands in an *I surrender* gesture. "Eight o'clock. Don't be late."

"Wish me luck," I murmur at the statue of the woman in the garden as I slip through the back door and try to climb as quietly as possible. But obviously, the statue has no luck to spare, because no sooner do I get to the kitchen door than it's flung open.

"Where have you been?" Rosie hisses. I'm standing two steps lower than her, so I tilt my head back and study her for a moment, without answering. Contrary to her furious words, her face is burning with some kind of inner glee.

"Visiting my dying aunt," I say, shouldering past her.

She blocks me. "I thought you didn't have any family."

I stop and consider this. "Right." My hair has come loose and is dripping down my neck, rivulets of water running past my shirt collar.

She steps closer, and I swear, she sniffs me. Then, her eyebrows curve up. "You wouldn't have been with a man, would you?" And now her voice is sly, teasing almost.

I shrug, attempt a half smile. "Don't tell anyone, Rosie," I whisper.

"I won't. But you owe me," she says, and gives me a little pinch on one arm as if to indicate that she'll collect.

"Rosie will be helping me to serve tonight," Mr. Tynsdell says in the kitchen after we've all consumed our hasty meal.

Except for Cook. She's probably had no time to eat all day, since she's still clattering pots and bustling over the stove, leaning in to check whatever's in there, a sour expression on her face.

But the rest of us have been lined up against the table as Mr. Tynsdell paces in front of us like a scarecrow version of a drill sergeant. "The rest of you," he adds with a jerk of his chin to include me, Lily, Dawn, and Tim, "will be clearing the dumbwaiter, handing up the new dishes, assisting Cook." He stops and sniffs at Tim. "Except for you. You will be in the stables." His nostrils dent and flare for a few seconds. "You smell of horses," he adds finally.

Tim scrubs at the back of his neck with one hand. "I do spend most of my time around them," he mutters, and Dawn gives a little giggle, which she chokes off when Mr. Tynsdell glares at her.

"See that you do not offend any of the Knight relatives with your . . . presence." He nods toward the door and Tim scurries out, no doubt considering himself lucky. "The rest of you have half an hour before you will be back here on duty. I expect all of you to look your best, even if you're going to be out of sight for the whole evening." At this he glares at Dawn, who reaches up one had to her hair as if to check that it's behaving. And with that, we're dismissed.

I follow Rosie to our room and divide my attention between watching the darkening street below the window and observing Rosie's last-minute preparations. First she unpins her hair and brushes it with quick, firm strokes. Her lips move as she counts to one hundred. Then with nimble fingers she pulls it all back up in an elegant twist, arranging her pins so that they're all invisible.

"Why bother with your hair, then?" I ask now as she fastens her white cap back in place until all of her hair is covered.

"I'd hardly expect you to know about these things," she says with a pointed glance at my own hair. It's dried from its earlier soaking, but I can feel it frizzing out around my ears. Still, I resist looking in the mirror or attempting to improve myself in any way. Not for the extended Knight family.

"So what are they like? The rest of the family?" I say now, staring out the window again.

At first, Rosie doesn't answer me and I look back at her, about to repeat my question. But she's sucking in her cheeks and applying powder to her cheekbones, so I wait. "Fascinating," she says at last. "All of them. So elegant and refined. The way real nobility should be."

I snort and then pretend to cough several times as Rosie glares at me. "Anyway," she says dreamily, "tonight is going to be very special."

Something about her tone puts me on guard, but I glance casually at her, then out the window again. Lights are flickering on in the brownstones opposite this one. "Really? Why?"

"Oh, just something Liam said. He said he might have something new for them to try." Rosie smiles at herself in the mirror, then dips her pinky finger in a little pot and dabs her lips with something crimson. "And he seems so excited."

The image of Liam filling the goblet with Alistair's blood flashes before my eyes.

I draw a breath. *Stick to the plan, Tam, stick to the stupid plan.*

Rosie stands and smoothes down the front of her dress. "Well, how do I look?"

"Beautiful," I say. Then I take three steps away from the window until I am standing directly in front of her. "Oh, wait, there's a little speck of something just above your eyebrow. Here, let me," I say before she can turn back to her mirror. I reach forward, my hand hovering over her eyes until both her eyelids flutter down.

"Hurry up, you—"

I tap my fingers on her forehead.

Please, please, please don't desert me.

Her stream of words chokes off. After a second, I maneuver her still-as-stone body to her bed and tip her in.

NINETEEN

"COOK, MR. TYNSDELL," I say, bursting into the kitchen. "Rosie fainted. We were upstairs and she just stood up and fainted. I put her in bed, but she's not feeling well at all." I make my eyes as wide as possible and look from one to the other.

"Lord have mercy," Cook gasps. "What are we—?"

Mr. Tynsdell's nostrils do their usual, predictable dance. "Unreliable. I should have known," he says quietly, and then draws himself upright, his eyes darting here and there as if assessing all his options. Finally, he looks at me. "Cook, see if you can rouse her, get her back on her feet. If you can't . . . You, girl"— and here he stabs a long finger at me. "You will assist me tonight."

I widen my eyes even further. "Yes, sir," I murmur. Cook throws one last look at the contents of the pot on the stove, from which a soft steam is wafting, then says sharply to Dawn, "Stir this. *Slowly*. If it starts to boil, you take it off the heat. Is that clear?" Reaching up to the top shelf, she pulls down a large, flat bottle, which she tucks into her apron pocket. Then she looks at Mr. Tynsdell, who nods as if releasing a general into battle, before bustling out of the kitchen. "I'll help her," I say, and dart after her before he can call me back.

Cook takes the stairs two at a time, and then trundles down the servants' hallway at an impressive speed. She's muttering all the while as she bursts into our room. "Rosie," she calls once, her voice sharp. Then she hurries over to the bed and bends over Rosie's still figure, slapping her cheeks softly. I'd tucked the covers over her, but now Cook pulls them back and slaps at Rosie's hands and arms before pulling the bottle from her pocket. She unscrews the cap, and the strong smell of alcohol fills the close air of the room. Tipping the bottle sideways, she angles some of the contents into Rosie's mouth. A thin stream of liquid dribbles right back out.

Cook blots it with her apron, then straightens up and looks at me. "What exactly happened here?" she says, still breathing heavily from climbing the stairs.

"I don't know," I say, circling my arms in the air. "One minute she was standing there and then she just fainted and I—"

"She seems dead," Cook says abruptly.

Carriage wheels creak by on the street below. Shouting and faint laughter drift through the thick windowpanes.

We stare at each other. "She's not dead, Cook," I say now. "She'll be all right."

Cook's labored breathing slows, softens. Her right hand darts up and makes the sign of the cross. "What did you do to her?"

I consider lying. But I don't. "Nothing permanent. But something that I had to do. I'll fix it later, I promise."

"Who are you?" Cook whispers. "From the moment you came here, I thought there was something different about you, and now . . ." She gestures back at Rosie.

"I thought you hated her anyway," I say, then immediately realize that's the wrong thing.

Cook blanches, makes the sign of the cross again. "You're just as bad as the rest of them."

"Who?"

"The Knight family. I can see plain as the eyes on my face that this girl didn't faint. She's under something, some kind of spell, and you . . . you . . ." Her words choke off and she turns, her shoulders stiff, moving toward the door.

"What do you care anyway?" I burst out. I indicate Rosie's body. "*She's helping them.* She brings children to Liam so he can experiment on them, and her uncle, or whoever he is, gets rid of their bodies. She *knew* Liam was killing the maids before me. She's awful."

But Cook knots her hands together around the bottle and says, without meeting my eyes, "It's not right what you did. She's . . . powerless against you, whoever you are. You're acting like them now."

"Cook," I say, and my voice rings out in the room. She stops but doesn't turn back to me. "I'm nothing like the Knight family. You have no way of knowing this, but really, I'm not. I'm . . . more like you."

Ordinary. Human.

And then again, I'm not.

"I promise Rosie will be okay, and . . ." I grope wildly for a second. "I'll help you, too. That statue in the backyard. If you tell me what happened maybe I can fix it—"

Cook turns, stares at me. "How do you know about that?"

I dig the tip of my boot into the floor. "I saw you one night. Talking to her. Her name is Mary, right? Who is she?"

Cook shudders, and then almost as an afterthought, she raises the bottle and takes a small swallow herself. "My sister," she says at last. "At one time I threatened to quit, to go to the police. This was after Tessa died—"

"Who's Tessa?" I whisper.

"The girl here before Livie."

"Liam got her too?"

Cook takes another swig, dabs away a drop from her lower lip with two fingers. "Bled her almost dry. She was a husk of a thing. Not even Lady Jessica could save her. Not after the third time. Not that she tried," Cook snorts. "So I said I was going to the police. The next day, Lady Knight brings me into her study. Says she has something special for me. Then she takes me out to the back garden. There's my sister standing there. And then they froze her. Right in front of me." She makes the sign of the cross again.

"La Spider did that?"

Cook stares at me. "Who?"

"Sorry, Lady Knight froze her. I didn't think she could—"

"No." Cook shakes her head. "It was her brother. Calvin Knight." She practically spits the name out. "He did it because she told him to. He just reached up and put his hand right over her heart"—she claps her own hand to her chest—"and then she was a great big stone. And they laughed and laughed while I cried. They told me that they could have done this to me, but that Lady Knight was too fond of my lemon soufflés. *Too fond of my lemon soufflés.*" She takes another swig from the bottle.

I draw in a breath to fight down the nausea surging inside me. And the anger. At the Knights for doing this, at my own family, who still wouldn't care if I told them this new evidence because after all, Cook and her sister are just Talentless humans. "I'm going to fix this," I mutter. "If it's the last thing I do in this stupid century, I'll fix this."

Cook blinks at me and I take the bottle from her outstretched fingers, take a gulp, then nearly choke. "What *is* this?" I gasp. The bridge of my nose feels like it's on fire.

"Not for beginners," she says, taking the bottle back from me. "You really can help me?"

I nod. "It might take some time, but yes."

She gives me a bleak look. "Time is all I have left. She was my only family." She studies my face for a moment. "If you're not like them, then what are you?"

I shrug. I have no way of answering that.

Mr. Tynsdell hisses a last-minute bout of instructions at me as he trims candlewicks and inspects the place settings for the seventeenth time. "Remember to serve on the left and clear from the right," he says while polishing a bone-handled carving knife with a handkerchief. "After the oysters and champagne are served, then . . ."

But I can barely listen to him. Instead, for probably the tenth time, I reach into my skirt pocket to check the time on the cameo watch that Jessica gave me. Seven o'clock. I have an hour and half before I have to let Gabriel in the side gate. I figure I can at least observe what the Knights are up to and maybe take this information along with the clock back to my family. Then they'll have to believe me.

Smoothing his mustache with his thumb and forefinger, Mr. Tynsdell gives me one last glance, and then says in his heavy voice, "I will make the announcement now." He sweeps from the room, his long narrow back like an exclamation point, and not for the first time do I wonder what keeps him here.

Candlesticks and white linen, crystal goblets and golden plates, all begin to blur before my eyes and for one second I wonder if I can claim that I caught Rosie's fainting disease. Then the door opens, and in this setting, once again, I am struck at how different a family dinner this is.

My family would be piling through the door, pushing and shoving, shouting good-naturedly, with Uncle Morris probably popping in and out of view, stepping on people's toes and apologizing before disappearing again. I could envision Aunt Beatrice darting around looking for an unattended wineglass, while Uncle Chester would be "accidentally" breaking something, much to my mother's annoyance, just so he could "fix" it. My father would be discussing his latest experiment with pea shoot grafting with anyone unlucky enough to be listening. James would be entwined around Rowena, his anchor, and last of all, my grandmother would be surveying everyone and everything so calmly, maybe closing one eye in her trademark wink.

Tomorrow night is Samhain, and I try not to think about how my family would be celebrating it. Then I give up and think about it anyway. Everyone would be gathered around the altar in the backyard and later there would be dancing around the bonfire. *There will be other festivals,* I remind myself fiercely, swallowing hard against the pain in my throat. *Gabriel will be able to find them again, he will.*

Then I stop thinking about Samhain and my family as La Spider enters the room, leading the procession of

Knights. She is escorted by a tall man with a thin mustache that looks sharp enough to cut. His dark eyes flick over me as if I'm part of the wall, and I wonder if this is Calvin Knight. Three more couples file in after them, the women all dressed in silk and taffeta and the men in dark suits with long waistcoats. Then a teenage boy and girl pass me, already looking bored, escorting an elderly woman between them. And finally, Jessica arrives, led in by Liam. Her round face is even paler than usual and her arm looks like it's been bolted to her brother's. Liam doesn't even acknowledge me. I assume he must have been with his mother when Mr. Tynsdell informed them that Rosie would not be assisting him that evening.

But they wouldn't have mentioned something so unimportant to Jessica, because her eyes pass over me, stop, and flicker back. An expression crosses her face briefly before her features resume their normal neutral mask, and so I'm left to puzzle over Jessica's look. A brief flash of what? Hope? But I don't have much time to think about it anyway, as Mr. Tynsdell's now signaling me. When everyone is seated, he begins to pour the champagne. I cross to the side table with two plates at a time and begin placing the raw oysters, still quivering slightly in their half shells, in front of each person. I serve Lady Knight first and then all the women, as he's instructed me, before the men.

When everyone is served, I retreat to the sideboard as expected, fold my hands behind my back, and wait.

La Spider holds her glass aloft. "Welcome, dearest family," she says. "It's a pleasure to be gathered here with you all tonight."

Candlelight shimmers and sprays across the crystal as twelve answering glasses are raised. Mr. Tynsdell twitches toward the champagne bottle as if already planning refills, and then the *clink* of forks and knives and conversation fill the room. The dumbwaiter rumbles and dishes appear, and my job is to unload them as fast and as silently as possible so Mr. Tynsdell can carry them off to the diners.

As the third course, what looks like tiny chickens in some sort of creamy-looking sauce, is cleared away, my heart begins to slow down to a normal rate. So far, the talk has been . . . ordinary. Ordinary nineteenth-century gossip. Politics, the state of the theater, and how dull the latest offering was at the Promenade. Delmonicos's new location and what it means for the rest of the city. The French singer, Marie Caitlin Amore, who was wearing almost nothing onstage and who apparently has a very rich politician in her pocket.

Tiny silver dishes of lemon ice garnished with curls of lemon peel appear in the dumbwaiter. I'm lifting them two at a time to the sideboard when La Spider raises her glass again and the room stills. All turn expectantly toward her. Except for Jessica, who stares down at her lap. For most of the evening she's pushed her knife and fork across the plate and eaten only air. Now La Spider says, "We've called you here tonight to witness something very special. As you know, my son, Liam, has long been striving to discover ways to deepen our Talents."

An excited murmur breaks across the table like a wave, and La Spider pauses gracefully, inclines her head toward Liam. My hands tremble as I stack the last of the filigreed salvers into the dumbwaiter. The plates sink out of view as either Dawn or Lily pulls the cord two flights below. Mr. Tynsdell appears at my side like a wisp of smoke to hand me a tray of silverware.

"Have you, Liam? Have you done it?" asks the man who escorted La Spider into the room. He leans across the table, his fingers toying with a silver serving spoon, bending and unbending the metal as if it's rubber.

La Spider flashes this man a look, as if annoyed by the interruption, but then she pauses and nods at her son.

"Well," Liam says, leaning back in his chair, "perhaps it's time for a little demonstration. Mother? What do you say?"

"Perhaps you're right," La Spider murmurs. Obviously, this has all been rehearsed between them.

Liam snaps his fingers, then looks at Mr. Tynsdell, who nods expressionlessly and leaves the room. The room swells with anticipation and I allow myself to scan each Knight family member's face. Eagerness, greed, anticipation dominate everyone's expression. Except for Jessica's. She presses her lips together in a bloodless white line.

All too soon, Mr. Tynsdell returns, followed by a small boy. I scan his face as he passes me, but it's not the same boy that I freed from here just last night. It's another child. Another, more unfortunate child. This one has at least the sense to be afraid, although who knows what they told him. His eyes are round and he stares at all of the faces that are turned so eagerly toward him. He is dressed in threadbare brown trousers and a shirt that's clearly too big for him. As the boy pushes his hair out of his eyes, his soiled gray sleeve falls back, revealing a bulky white bandage wrapped around one wrist.

"Come here, child," Liam says in a kind avuncular tone.

Run, I want to scream. Instead, I lock the scream inside my throat and try to keep my face blank. The child pauses, one foot digging into the thick golden carpet, and then he moves forward, his eyes fixed on Liam's face. Leaning back in his chair, Liam produces a small bottle from his coat pocket and pours half of it into his wineglass. He pours the remaining half into another glass and hands that one to the child. After dipping one hand in his pocket, he pulls out a small blue bottle and shakes it over his own glass until a few drops fall into the wine.

The man across the table from Liam opens his mouth, but La Spider puts her hand on his arm and he leans back. Silently, he wraps the handle of the silver spoon around and around his thumb, his eyes watchful.

Next, Liam lifts his own glass in a mocking toast and says gently, "To your health," before draining it.

The child stares at his wineglass as if he's never held something that fine before.

"Come, come, drink it all up, like I told you," Liam says, and winks at the table in general. But the child still hesitates, his eyes flickering around the room.

The elderly woman stirs and hisses, "Drink it, you little—" but one of the other women whispers something too soft for me to catch and the elderly woman subsides, her mouth bunching into a hard knot.

"Come along," Liam says in a still-jovial tone, although now a thread of steel runs through it.

"What about the dollar?" the child says at last, his voice rough and harder than expected. He juts his shoulders forward like a boxer.

"You'll have your money, never fear," Liam says, and then spreads his hands wide to the table. "A little entrepreneur, we have here."

"Indeed," La Spider murmurs, her fingers tightening on her own glass.

Do something! I scream silently at Jessica, but she never raises her eyes from her lap.

The boy sips at his glass. He makes a grimace and jerks his head away, but Liam says softly, "All of it. That was the deal."

The rest of the liquid disappears down the boy's throat.

He swallows, shudders, and then wipes his mouth with the back of his hand before saying, "My money?"

There is a sharp swell of silence, and then almost imperceptibly the boy's hand begins to tremble. His face draws into a knot and then he opens his mouth as if he's about to be sick on the carpet.

"Easy now," Liam murmurs, and all at once the boy's face smoothes out and he turns blank eyes on Liam, who leans back in his chair, a small smile playing around his lips.

The silence in the room is overwhelming.

"Boy," Liam says softly, "I want you to turn in a circle three times."

Obediently, the child shuffles his feet until he has come about-face. He does it twice more, then stops and looks at Liam with a waiting expression. "Excellent," Liam murmurs. "And now walk over to that side of the room and keep walking until I say stop."

The child turns again and begins heading toward the wall with precise, easy steps. As he passes me, his eyes are alert, focused, and it's clear that he has no intention of stopping. As he comes within three feet, then two feet of the wall, Liam strokes his mustache thoughtfully but remains silent. The boy's forehead makes contact with the wall with a sickening thud and as he stumbles and falls to the floor. Titters fill the room.

"Astounding," says one of the men who followed

behind La Spider and her escort. He steeples his fingers on his chin, his eyes darting between Liam and the child on the floor.

One of the Knight teenagers pipes up. "Make him do it again."

"No, make him take off all his clothes," the girl interjects with a giggle. She stands up and says in a pretty good imitation of La Spider's tone, "Take off your clothes."

But the boy, still sprawled on the floor, ignores her, rubbing his forehead.

The girl sits back down, looking crestfallen. "Why won't he do it, Cousin Liam?"

Liam smiles at her fondly, a smile that doesn't reach his eyes. "Because he'll listen to me only. I've mixed his blood and mine in the spell, so only I can control him."

A soft murmur breaks out and then the Knight boy leans forward with a glinting smile. "I want one, too," he says to the woman I presume is his mother. She smiles down at him brightly and says, "Soon enough, Edmund. Uncle Liam will show us how." Then she aims an arch glance across the table. "Won't you, darling? So we can all have . . . a little pet?"

But it's La Spider who answers. "As usual you fail to grasp what's happening, Clarissa." Clarissa's face flushes and her fingers flutter up to her pearl necklace, but she remains silent. "We do not do this so we can all have *little pets* for our own personal amusement."

"How long will it last?" asks the second man, the one with the golden handlebar mustache who escorted Clarissa into the room. There's something similar to La Spider in the set of his chin and the way they both turn their heads in whiplike movements.

Liam shrugs. "Not long, but as long as it's renewed, he'll remain under my control."

"And will it work on one of us?" the man asks, his voice trembling a little.

Liam's chair creaks loudly as he straightens up. He exchanges a look with his mother. "So suspicious, Calvin," La Spider says with a small smile flitting across her lips.

I stare at the man. So that's Calvin Knight.

"I was just about to get to that," Liam says softly.

"Do you see, Clarissa?" La Spider chides.

"Yes," Clarissa breathes, and then makes a preemptory movement to shush her son, who has opened his mouth again.

"It will."

There is a collective gasp around the table. I drop my own gaze to the floor, studying the dark inlaid squares of wood, but my head is spinning.

"How did you learn this?" Calvin Knight asks, his eyes darting from his sister's face to Liam's. I try to figure out if it's fear or greed in his expression. "Who . . . volunteered to . . ." His eyes fasten on Jessica now.

Liam laughs. "Oh, no. I didn't experiment on anyone

you know. We don't experiment on each other. Unless anyone would like to volunteer?" No one replies except for Clarissa, who gives a small, nervous titter. La Spider's eyes dart to her and Clarissa flushes and looks down at her fingers gripping the table, her sleeve almost dipping into her dish of melting lemon ice.

"I would," Jessica says suddenly. Everyone's head swivels to her. I fight to keep my gaze neutral.

"Jessica," Liam begins with a smile playing across his full lips. But the look she sends him blasts the smile from his face.

"I would let you drain me of my blood as long as it would drain all my Talent away. But somehow I doubt that you really want the ability to heal people, Liam. That's not your specialty, is it?" Her tone is icy, mocking.

"Oh, I don't know about that," Liam murmurs. "It could prove useful." He nods toward the child, who appears to be unconscious, on the floor. "But it's not necessary. For now," he drawls, and something about the way he says it makes me very afraid. "Just recently we had a visitor. A very special visitor. He proved to be more useful than I ever could have imagined. Allow me to introduce our next guest." He gives another nod to Mr. Tynsdell, who exits the room once again.

Suddenly, it feels as if the walls are pressing in on me.

As if locked in a bad dream, I watch the door swing open and Mr. Tynsdell return followed by a shuffling, stumbling figure. A bandage is wrapped around the man's head, and both of his arms are encased in gauze. He licks his lips once and scans the room, taking in all of the Knights, who are staring back at him.

I edge backwards until I bump into the wainscoting on the wall. Looking left, I calculate the distance to the still-open door. About twenty feet.

Just when I'm weighing my odds of sprinting out of here, the man turns his face in my direction. Those blue-gray eyes burn right into me.

"Tamsin Greene," Alistair hisses.

TWENTY

FOR THREE HEARTBEATS the room is still and then Liam pushes back his chair and says, "Who?" just as Alistair flings his arm out toward me and screams, *"That's her. She's here. I told you she's here."*

"Who *is* this madman?" Calvin Knight says, also coming to his feet to stand next to Liam. "And what is he talking about?"

Behind Alistair's shoulder I see Liam stare at me and then gather himself as if he's about to spring. My skin suddenly tingles. But Liam remains solid. And very surprised.

Thank you, thank you, thank you. That was the third time.

La Spider flings up one hand and the door suddenly slams shut.

So much for that exit.

I take a step closer to the sideboard and the dumbwaiter. In my peripheral vision, the rest of the Knight family is coming to their feet, and voices begin to buzz through the room. But Alistair only has eyes for me.

"You won't succeed, Tamsin," Alistair says, his voice hoarse. His lips are dry and cracked, and the whites of his eyes have taken on a yellow tinge. "It's too late. I've made sure of that. I've saved my family."

I note the half-empty champagne bottle within reach and try to gauge how hard I could hit someone with it. "And look how they rewarded you!" I indicate his bandaged head and arms. "By practically killing you."

"Apparently, you don't understand what it means to sacrifice for your family."

"I understand—"

"My Talent is gone." He raises pole-thin arms and shows me the fresh scabs crisscrossing his skin. "It's been bled away. But I don't mind. As long as it's helped my family to understand their true potential, their truth worth."

His words have shaken me more than I want to admit.

"Not that you'll be around to see it." I inject a breezy note into my voice as I add, "It's been three days for you, hasn't it? You've got what, hours to live?"

"Enough," La Spider says, breaking our locked gazes.

"This is the girl you were warning us about? The maid? *She's* a member of the Greene family?" Liam says, studying me with something close to amusement.

"Took you long enough," I say, mostly to drag the

smirk off of this face. "I've been in your house for almost three days. You guys are kind of pathetic."

La Spider tightens her lips and flings up her hand again. A sharp prickling washes over me, followed by that super sense of clarity.

I smile sweetly at her. "Still here."

"Kill her," the old woman hisses just as Clarissa disappears. I reach out with my mind and snap her back into sight. Next to her, her son flickers and then stretches, growing larger and larger by the second until his head's about to bump into the ceiling. He cracks his knuckles and begins lumbering toward me.

"Stop it," I say almost kindly to him, and with a quick snap he shrinks back down to his normal size. Too bad I couldn't keep going until he was the size of a pencil.

"Don't use your Talent on her," Alistair roars just as La Spider shrieks, "Enough!"

"This is truly fortunate," Liam purrs into the silence. He places a hand on his mother's arm. "We were going to start *selecting* members of the Greene family as it was. But now one has fallen into our laps." He smiles warmly at the rest of his family. "As I was about to demonstrate with our honored guest here"—he nods to Alistair—"I have discovered how to borrow someone else's Talent. Of course, the process still needs a little refining, but now that we have her—"

"I don't think I'll be sticking around for that," I interject.

"Oh, really?" Liam says coldly, and now there's no amusement in his voice whatsoever. Behind his back, Jessica is staring at me. She looks afraid, but I can't tell if it's of me or for me. "I'm afraid you don't have a choice in that matter."

"Restrain her," La Spider says to Mr. Tynsdell.

I glance sideways at the butler, who is hesitating.

"Now," La Spider says, her voice like a whiplash.

I have a second to feel almost sorry for him as he comes toward me. He raises his arms to grab me. Twisting sideways, I evade his grasp and slap him on the forehead.

A terrified expression crosses his face and he jumps back as if I've burned him. He scrubs his hand across his forehead.

Great. Perfect time for Aunt Beatrice's power to desert me.

The rumble of the dumbwaiter rising behind me shatters the silence.

"Seize her," La Spider calls again, and this time Calvin Knight moves forward.

Rage has tightened his mouth into a snarling knot. "You little b—"

Gathering myself, I coalesce into what feels like a ball of energy, and then I dive straight into Calvin Knight's chest. With a flash, my flesh evaporates, my sight dulls, and I feel a pulling sensation as if a strong wind could suddenly scatter me into a thousand pieces.

And then I am solid again.

"What happened?" Clarissa shrieks just as Alistair stumbles forward.

"She's inside of him," he says hoarsely.

The entire room erupts into pandemonium.

"Get her," La Spider shrieks again, clenching her hands together as if to prevent herself from flinging me/her brother against the wall.

La Spider's other brother darts forward and drives his head into my chest. I struggle away from him long enough to grab the champagne bottle. With a wide swing, I manage to clobber the side of his face. He grunts and steps back, and that's all the space I need. Moving as fast as I can in my new body, I throw myself into the dumbwaiter shaft and pull the rope.

Hurry, hurry, hurry.

Thankfully, each servant in this horrible house has learned to move with a clockwork precision. With a creaking groan, the dumbwaiter platform begins to descend through the dark shaft into the kitchen below.

With a crash the dumbwaiter stops in the kitchen. Dawn, her arms coated in a thin gray film of soapsuds, turns from the sink and starts toward me, intending no doubt to take the next load of dirty dishes. Instead, she stops short, staring at me, her hands dripping water across the stone floor. Abruptly she claps one wet hand over her mouth. A sort of moan leaks out between her fingers.

"Hi, Dawn," I say, scrambling off the platform and knocking aside a dish. Calvin Knight's dark evening suit is blotched with the remains of dinner. Good.

At the sound of a male voice, Cook whirls from the stove, her silver whisk clutched in her right hand. Her eyes widen.

"Cook, it's me, Tam . . . er . . . Agatha. Seriously, it's me. It's not him. Sorry about crashing in on you guys here. Tell them I went out the front door."

Even now I can hear voices above our heads somewhere calling. *"Lock the doors,"* La Spider is screaming, and then there's an answering shout.

Cook crosses herself with the whisk still in her hand as I thud down the back stairs.

"How did you . . . are you . . . is it—? Wait!" she calls.

Fumbling with the latch, I throw one look over my shoulder.

"My sister," she implores. Her eyebrows slant upward in such a desperately hopeful expression that I bite my lip.

"Elements," I mutter, flinging the door open.

Behind me, Cook cries out, "You promised."

An almost full moon sails across the sky, shining down on the stone woman trapped in the garden. Sprinting across the frozen grass, I skid to a stop before her. "Please let this work." My breathing comes in ragged gulps as I slap one hand down onto where the woman's heart should be.

A pulse abruptly kicks to life under my fingertips, and the cold stone heats to hot skin so fast that I jerk my hand away. The statue lifts her head and blinks her eyes, and even in the bleach-colored light I can see that blood is rushing to fill her cheeks. With an audible popping noise, she stumbles toward me, her arms pinwheeling. Terror spasms across her features like a tidal wave.

The door creaks open behind me and I jump, but it's only Cook, still carrying her whisk, and hurrying across the grass to us. "Mary?" Cook whispers, and the woman swings her head toward her sister.

"Matilda," she says in a creaking voice as if stone dust has clogged her throat.

"Oh, thank God, thank God," Cook sobs. Dropping her whisk, she runs forward, and the two women careen into each other's arms. Looking up, I can see lights flooding through the windows of each room on the second and third floors. The hunt's in earnest.

"Take my advice?" I say to both of them. "Leave this house. Now." Without waiting for an answer, I dart across the lawn. Peering through the side gate, I check out the street beyond it. Empty.

I ease open the gate as quietly as I can. Still, it makes

a creaking noise that sets me to grinding Calvin Knight's back teeth. Inching down the walkway, I listen as hard as I can. There's a shout in the distance, a burst of laughter from a small group of passersby, and then the sound of carriage wheels rolling down Twenty-seventh Street. All the normal night noises.

My fingers work the latch as quickly as possible, and then I open the gate door just enough to slip through. I figure I have just enough time to find Gabriel and have him help me figure out a way to slip out of Calvin Knight's body and then—

Pain explodes across the left side of my face.

I stagger backwards, my body falling through the half-open gate. Black spots weave and dance across my vision and slowly coalesce into the form of Liam Knight. He is standing over me, wielding an iron poker.

"Sorry, *Uncle*," Liam says, his voice not sounding sorry at all. I shake Calvin Knight's head, but that only makes things worse. Blood is trickling down my jaw, and seems to be pooling in my ear.

"It couldn't be helped," La Spider says, emerging from the shadows to stand next to her son. She studies my/her brother's body with merciless eyes. "Calvin will just have to understand."

"He doesn't seem like the understanding type," I mutter, or try to anyway, but my words come out all slurry. The black spots are getting worse, although oddly enough one of them seems shaped like a crow. A small crow perched on the stone banister just above Liam and La Spider's heads.

"Isobel," I gasp. "Help me."

La Spider's eyes narrow and then she glances upward. Instantly the crow takes flight, but La Spider jabs one finger at it.

"No," I scream. I reach out with my mind to snap off La Spider's Talent, but my reflexes are just seconds too slow.

The crow's body slams once, twice in a first-floor casement window and then flops to the pavement below. Slowly, the bird's body shifts into Isobel's supine form. One dark feather drifts gently downward to land in her outstretched right hand.

"Well, well, what a harvest," Liam murmurs.

I do the only thing left that I can do. I black out.

TWENTY-ONE

HEAT THROBS THROUGH MY jaw. An answering throb in my temple almost makes me moan, but somehow I manage to stifle it. Keeping my eyes closed, I try to take a quick inventory. I'm sitting upright and what feels like ropes are digging into the skin on my wrists. I seem to be tied to a hard-backed chair. There is a crack and a pop. It sounds like a log has shifted in a fireplace. I have to be in either Liam's or La Spider's study. Risking a quick peek through nearly closed eyelids, I confirm that yes, it's Liam's study, and yes, Isobel is tied up in a chair next to me. I shift my mostly closed eyes to the wall where the clock once hung. It's gone. With a jolt I remember Alistair's gloating words at the dinner. *"You won't succeed. I've made sure of that."*

Never mind. Gabriel can find it again and then—

Gabriel! I'm not there to let him in the side gate and now he's going to be walking into danger at any minute.

Snapping my eyes open, I confirm that it's just me and Isobel in the room. An unconscious Isobel.

"Isobel," I whisper, rocking my chair back and forth until it's closer to hers. "Wake up. We have to get out of here." There's a faint blue shadow forming on her right temple, and I'll bet she has a headache to match mine. "Isobel," I hiss, and this time her eyes snap open. She studies my face, frowning.

"It's me, Tamsin. I'm in Calvin Knight's body, but I swear it's me."

She swallows once as if trying to get rid of an unpleasant taste in her mouth, then nods at me. "I saw what they did, before . . . I fell?"

"La Spider got you. I'm sorry. I was too slow. What the hell were you doing out there anyway?" I flex my fingers against the rope. Too tight.

Her eyelids flutter closed, then open again. Color is slowly seeping back into her cheeks as she takes in her surroundings. "Thom, my grandfather, sent me here. To find you."

"Thom sent you? That doesn't make any sense. Why?" Why would he put his granddaughter in danger? Then I decide that since my own grandmother frequently seems to fling me into dangerous situations, it must be a Greene family trait.

Her lips flicker into a wry twist. "Often what he does makes very little sense. To other people." She shakes her head, then winces, seeming to regret that she did that. "Something he read in the book made him send me here.

No one else knows. They wouldn't have let me come. The others . . ."

"Cera and her brothers?"

She nods. "They still don't believe that the Knights will—"

But she stops speaking at the sound of raised voices in the hallway.

"Why?" Someone is sobbing, and after a second, I recognize Clarissa's voice. A steel murmur overrides it. La Spider.

"Hurry," I whisper. "Can you—?"

But I don't need to even finish my sentence. Lightning fast, she's morphed into a crow. Fluttering free of the ropes, the bird hops to the floor, one wing dragging a little. And then as quickly, she turns back into a human. Stumbling to her feet, she kneels behind my chair. Her fingers scrabble against my skin, picking away at the knots in the ropes. Throwing another look at the partially open door, I whisper, "We have to hurry. There's a secret passageway here. Just before we get in there, I think the best thing is for me to come out of Calvin's body and then—"

"What an excellent idea. I believe my uncle would appreciate that," a soft voice purrs.

Both Isobel and I jerk upright. Liam's standing in the doorway. And next to him is La Spider. Her eyes glitter and her white face seems to gleam with a cold triumph. But my eyes can only focus on the small silver revolver that she's pointing directly at us.

TWENTY-TWO

IN A VOICE LIKE A STEEL trap, she says, with a nod toward Isobel, "Move. Toward the other side of the room."

Isobel hesitates, then stands slowly, and moves a few steps away toward the fireplace. The muzzle of the gun tracks her progress. "If you try anything. Anything at all, I will shoot her." La Spider says to me. I study her milk white face and decide she's serious, so I nod. Then again, I don't have much of a choice.

"Trust me, she's an excellent shot. As my father could have attested had he lived to tell the tale," Liam says.

"Charming family," I murmur, but La Spider ignores that.

"You will come out of my brother on the count of three. Is that clear? Again, if you attempt in any way to—"

"I got it," I snap, furiously trying to come up with a brilliant plan in all of three seconds that doesn't involve getting shot.

"Now," La Spider says, and she clicks back the hammer on her revolver. "One, two, three."

"Okay, okay," I whisper. Closing Calvin's eyes, I grope upward. It's like reaching for a shaft of light on the surface of water.

"Ugh," Calvin groans as I stumble to the floor. La Spider trains her gun on me.

"Trust me, I felt the same way about you," I mutter, rubbing the side of my face. In the middle of all this, I note that even back in my own body, I still feel the pain in my jaw from when Liam hit Calvin's face with the poker.

"Why am I tied up? What has happened?" Then Calvin's eyes light on mine. "You!" he hisses. "You . . ."

"It's over, Uncle," Liam says, hurrying forward. With swift fingers he unknots the ropes and helps his uncle stand. Calvin touches his jaw, winces, then starts toward me. But Liam steps in between us and wheels his uncle toward the door. "And now, perhaps it's best if you comfort your wife. She'll be very glad to see you . . . returned to yourself, so to speak."

"Lavinia," Calvin says in a tight voice. "What exactly is going on here? Who is this guttersnipe and how did she—"

"We'll speak tomorrow," La Spider says. And even though they're worlds apart, there's something in the finality of her tone that reminds me of my grandmother at her most impassive. Calvin blinks once, touches his jaw again. Then he looks at me one last time before leaving the room. He slams the door shut behind him.

"Don't move," La Spider snaps at me, her gun trained on Isobel's heart. I settle back down from my attempt to get to my feet. Isobel and I exchange glances.

"Why not just kill us now?" Isobel asks, and I have to admire the pitch-perfect scorn in her voice, even though I can see that her lips are trembling.

"Because Liam likes to play with his food first," I answer her.

Liam gives me his lazy perfect smile.

"Agatha," he purrs. "Excuse me. Tamsin. If only I had known you were so . . . feisty." Moving briskly to his desk, he presses a small black button that I know will ring a bell through the servants' quarters.

"Rosie won't be coming," I tell him. "If that's who you're calling. She's frozen at the moment." I decide not to tell him that it'll wear off in a week or so. At least according to what my Aunt Beatrice always claimed.

Liam tugs on his lip thoughtfully. "You are going to be such a fascinating creature to study."

La Spider frowns at me.

I pin my eyes on the revolver that La Spider is now holding so steadily on Isobel and gather myself silently. If I can jump into La Spider and point the gun at Liam, somehow we can—

A loud banging shatters my focus. A loud banging followed by the pealing of the front doorbell over and over.

La Spider and Liam exchange glances. Although her gun never wavers, any remaining color drains from her face.

"Whoever it is—" Liam begins.

"It's obviously them," La Spider hisses. "I knew this was not a good—"

"Trust in me, Mother," Liam hisses back. If the situation weren't so dire, I'd be fascinated by this apparent schism between them.

"Sirs," Mr. Tynsdell's voice rises. "This is a most inappropriate hour. No one . . . young man, where are you going? *Stop at once.* I—"

Isobel turns her face to mine and I can see the question in her eyes.

His voice is cut off as Liam shuts the door, turns the silver key in the lock, and pockets it.

"Gabriel," I scream. "Up here. We're up here." As La Spider swings the gun on me, I duck and pull Isobel down with me just as she changes into a crow and half flutters, half flies toward the window.

With deadly aim, La Spider points her gun at the winging black crow and pulls the trigger. The bullet slams into the wall a second after Isobel banks sharply left and flies directly at La Spider's face. La Spider takes two steps back, flinging up one arm protectively as Liam begins to shimmer and fade.

"No, you don't," I whisper. Reaching out, I pull hard.

His form becomes solid again and he swings his head directly to me. "So, that's what you can do," he says softly. "Oh, how I will enjoy taking that."

"I'd like to see you try," I snarl, shoving myself to my feet.

"Tamsin," Gabriel shouts from outside the room just as there is a tremendous crash against the wooden door. Followed by another. And then a third. At that the door splinters just as Isobel's crow form is suddenly hurtled with an awful speed against the wall. There is a sickening thud and then the bird slides down the wall to huddle at the foot of the fireplace.

"Isobel," I scream, and run to her. Slowly she morphs into her human form again, but her eyes remain closed. Blood seeps from her lower lip.

"Don't move," I hear La Spider say in her chilling voice, and I look up to see Gabriel standing in the doorway. His eyes find mine and I nod. He jerks his chin back at me before turning to face La Spider and her gun, which is pointed directly at his head. Gabriel puts his hands up, but he adopts more of a boxing stance than an "I surrender" one. As La Spider's gaze rakes over him, I notice Mr. Tynsdell hovering in the hallway.

"Sir," he begins. "Shall I . . ."

La Spider flicks her free hand toward him. "Dismissed," she says almost absently. He scurries away.

Liam looks from Gabriel to me, raising one eyebrow. "And just who is this? Oh, how the puzzle deepens."

Before I can reply, a gentle voice filters through the doorway. "Really, Lavinia. Has it come to this?" And with that Thom steps into the room, shouldering Gabriel lightly aside with his cane. He is dressed in a perfectly pressed dark suit and his hair is combed neatly back on his head, almost as if he has an important appointment.

A chill breaks out across my skull. Thom Greene seems unfazed that he's standing in the Knight house. In fact, he seems determined.

La Spider draws herself upright. "Thom Greene," she says softly. Gabriel begins to inch sideways along the wall toward me, always keeping his eyes on La Spider, but she seems to have forgotten him for the moment.

Thom inclines his head. "Yes. It has been a number of years. And I see that we must meet again under these most unfortunate circumstances."

For once, La Spider seems at a loss for words as an almost panicked expression flits across her face. Her eyes dart wildly to Liam as if seeking reassurance. Again, I wonder who convinced whom to start experimenting on the Greenes. And then Cera's words come back to me: *La Spider called my mother a fool, but she left. More importantly, she left us alone. And we've lived in peace ever since.*

Apparently, that peace is about to change, thanks to Liam.

Isobel stirs in my arms and struggles to sit up. "Grand-father," she whispers. At the sight of the blood on her face, Thom's expression hardens.

"What were you planning to do with her?" he says soft-ly. All traces of gentleness have vanished from his voice.

Liam shrugs, smiles lazily. "Why don't you ask her? She's the one who came to this house. In disguise."

Thom nods slowly. "Perhaps. But do you deny that you have been following us, studying us for weeks?" He pauses for a courteous moment, and when Liam doesn't answer, he nods. "Of course you don't." He takes another step into the room, closer to Isobel and me. But he keeps his gaze on Liam's face and I'm suddenly reminded of a professor schooling an errant pupil. "For what purpose, may I ask? Why have you been so suddenly interested in us? Did we not have a pact? To leave each other alone?"

La Spider swallows, her long throat seeming to con-vulse, but it's Liam who answers. "Times change, old man. We're only doing what you yourself would have done soon-er or later."

Thom shakes his head. "I think not. We Greenes are not quite as fixated on blood as you are."

"You Greenes are fools, then," Liam murmurs. "And I for one do not intend to suffer a fool." And with a motion almost too swift to follow he draws a shining silver knife from his coat and plunges it into Thom's side.

Next to me, Isobel jumps as if she herself has been stabbed. "Grandfather," she screams. Thom turns his head to her, gives a long look, and then almost in slow motion begins to crumple and fall. As he does so, he lifts one hand and the lights go out, plunging the room into darkness. At almost the same time, a tingle slips over my skin. Either Liam or La Spider just attempted to use their power on me.

"Tam," Gabriel shouts, but then it sounds as if my name has been abruptly choked out of his throat. In the dim light filtering from the window I see Liam and Gabriel wrestling each other for the knife. A flash of silver, then someone grunts. I struggle to pull Isobel to her feet.

"Come on, we've got to get out of here," I murmur as the gun goes off over our heads and shatters the window behind us.

"Not without my grandfather," Isobel sobs into my ear.

In the dim street light coming in the windows, I see La Spider raise her gun and point it directly at me just as Gabriel and Liam crash into her. Liam's outline suddenly begins to waver and shift.

"Tamsin," Gabriel yells again. This time I reach out and pull hard on Liam and he solidifies again, panting. In the second that Liam takes to catch his breath, Gabriel swiftly kicks his legs out from under him and punches him once, twice, in the face.

With a shriek, La Spider points her hand at Gabriel,

and this time I'm not fast enough. Gabriel's body is suddenly flung halfway across the room. With a grunt, he collides into the leather armchair and slides to the floor.

Tugging Isobel with me, I stumble to his side. "Gabriel," I cry. "Are you—"

He snaps open his eyes and I swear they're blazing at me in the shadows of the room. "Don't resist this," he growls, and he clamps his fingers around my wrist so tightly that I'm sure I'll be wearing a bracelet of bruises for days to come. With his other hand, he catches hold of Isobel's upper arm.

"Not without Thom," I cry. Stretching forward with all my might, I lock my fingers into the old man's just as La Spider aims the gun at my chest and pulls the trigger.

But the gunshot never comes. I flinch anyway as La Spider's shriek bursts against my ears. The sound goes on and on even as darkness and light whirl past me in a kaleidoscope until finally it thins out into a hollow keening moan.

I open my eyes. A cold wind whips past my ears and the ground underneath me is hard. Here and there crusts of old snow cover the yellowed meadow like so many scabs. A tall gray house looms before me, but its shutters are broken and banging in the wind against the peeling, burnt walls.

Gabriel keeps one hand locked around my wrist but releases Isobel as she sits up. "Where are we?" she whispers.

"Hedgerow," I say bleakly. I consider the shell of the house in front of me. The last time I saw it, it was full of light and people and life. "What used to be my home."

"It was the only place I could think of fast enough," Gabriel says. "Even though I knew it wasn't . . . the way we left it. I couldn't find that." He runs his fingers over his lower lip, dabbing away a trickle of blood.

"Are you hurt?" I ask, checking the rest of his face for bruises, but he shakes his head, so I turn my attention to Thom. With two quick jerks, Isobel has torn off the hem of her petticoat and is wadding the material into Thom's side. But from the expression on her face, she seems to think it's hopeless. Still, her voice is steady when she looks at me and says, "We need to get him back home. Cera can heal him. She knows . . . remedies. She can—" Her voice chokes off as Thom reaches up one shaking hand and touches her mouth gently. His eyelids flicker open.

"It's too late for that," he whispers. He shifts and tries to sit up.

"Don't," Isobel cries, her fingers working faster to stanch the bleeding.

"Young man," Thom says, "help me sit up."

Gabriel hesitates, looks at Isobel for a split second, and then puts his arm around Thom's shoulder and props him up halfway. "Sir, I think—"

"Shhh," Thom says, and we all fall silent as he turns his

head left and right to take in the meadow and the remains of the house. "This is a good place," he whispers at last. "A strong place. I can feel the elements here."

I stare at the shell of the house. "It was—" I say, and suddenly tears escape my eyes and the pain in my throat is too great for any more words.

Thom looks at me calmly. "And it will be again, Tamsin. You have to be brave. And you have to make a choice. A terrible choice," he whispers.

I rub my forehead with the heels of my palms to ease away a sudden headache. "Not that again," I mutter.

"Always that, I'm afraid."

He turns to Isobel, blots the tears that are streaming down her face with his fingertips. "And you, too, must be brave. Read the book. But do not let it overwhelm you." There is a sharp hitch in his breath. "It is to be used as a guide only."

"Why did you send me there?" Isobel murmurs brokenly. "To that awful place? If you knew this would happen? If you knew you were going to die?"

A ghost of a smile crosses Thom's lips. "Only the very young seem to think that we can avoid death. We cannot. We can only perhaps choose how we meet it." He takes another wincing breath and the lines around his eyes suddenly tighten. "This is a fine place. Bury me here."

Isobel makes a startled sound of protest, but he only repeats, "Bury me here and build the altar over me. Perhaps we will come here." Then he smiles at me. "Again."

TWENTY-THREE

THE SOUND OF SILVIUS'S howling seems to ring through the Greenes' house even though Isobel and her wolf have fled to the woods. An hour ago Gabriel, Isobel, and I Traveled back. But before doing that, in my time we buried Thom in the meadow behind the ruined hulk of what had once been my family's house. It had taken the better part of three hours to finally hack a deep enough hole in the semi-frozen ground and place Thom's body in it. And all the while, Isobel hadn't made a single sound, but the tears had run freely down her cheeks as the three of us stood over the makeshift grave. Finally, she joined hands with the both of us and led us in the traditional prayer for a soul's release, and if the harmony of our three voices seemed weak and thin under the rising wind, she didn't protest. Then, with our hands still locked, Gabriel had taken us back to 1887 to Isobel's home. In that front room where we first met Cera, her brothers, and Thom, we explained what had happened at the Knight house to Cera, Philben, and Phineaus.

And then with a single glance between them, Philben and Phineaus had gone to summon the rest of the Greene family home to keep them safe. Isobel had left the room abruptly, her fingers wound tightly in Silvius's fur, while Cera, Gabriel, and I sat in silence as the firelight shifted and dimmed into darkness.

Finally, Cera stirs, crosses to the side table, and begins to fiddle with the wick on an oil lamp. Under her fingers, the light from the lamp begins to grow and cast golden shadows across the plain white walls. Only then does she turn to face us again, and it's then that I can see her eyes are swollen. With a pang, I recall Thom's Talent to bring light or darkness to any room.

Another mournful howl echoes from the woods. Right about now I feel like pressing my hands over my ears and screaming, too.

But instead I pick and choose among the hundred questions that are jostling for first place. "Do you believe us now?" I whisper.

Cera seems to be holding herself very still, as if she's afraid she's going to break into a hundred pieces. But she manages to nod. "It was never a question of believing you or not believing you," Cera says finally. The flames in the oil lamp seem to quiver in response.

Could have fooled me. But I decide not to say this out loud, and Cera continues.

"It was a question of how to respond to your warning."

I take a breath. All at once her eyes flood with tears and guilt twists across her face, so I bite down on whatever I was going to say.

"He knew what was coming and he still let it happen. In fact, he went out and met it deliberately." Her mouth twists downward. "What's the good of being able to read the future if you can't prevent anything like this?" she whispers, her words stirring the still air of the room.

Hesitantly, I say, "He told me that dying is never a choice."

Cera removes her hand, blinks at me. I can't tell if this is any comfort to her or not. She shakes her head, then says in a stronger voice, "Now we have to make sure that he didn't die in vain. And that he's not buried . . . there . . . alone. Forever."

I nod. "We need to make the Domani. We need . . . needed the clock that I told you about. The one hanging in the Knight house. But Alistair, I think he already had them destroy it."

I turn to Gabriel. "Can you find it at all?"

He closes his eyes briefly, then shakes his head. "It's gone."

I shiver. The skin under his eyes has taken on a darker tinge. It's the night of the second day. He doesn't have much time left. *Think, think, think.* "The Domani," I repeat doggedly, hoping some flash of an idea will come to me. "We need to make sure that it's done differently this time. Last time it was . . . an imperfect solution, as my grandmother put it."

"Blood," says a voice, and all three of us jump. Isobel is standing in the door. In the lantern light, her face is all hard planes and angles. Silvius stands at her side, watching all of us with narrow golden eyes.

"We'll make certain it's done right. The Knights are not the only ones who understand the power of blood spells."

"Isobel," Cera murmurs, but the younger woman's face is resolute.

"*I don't care.* After what that man did . . . to Grandfather. I don't care how much of their blood we spill." She buries long white fingers in the fur at Silvius's neck.

"We are not going to spill blood," Cera says sharply. "That is not what we—"

"Oh, but we will," Isobel says softly. Then she straightens up, opens her mouth, and says in a singsong, eerie voice, "One stood for North and one stood for South. One stood for East, and one stood for West. And one stood Center. North summoned Air, and South carried Water, East called Fire, and West brought Earth." She pauses. "And the Center offered blood. And all bound together."

I feel a chill break out across my arms as the words of the Domani spell spill forth from her lips.

"I read it," Isobel says. "For the first time tonight, it appeared in the book." White lines bracket her mouth as if she's clenching her back teeth to keep from screaming. "The fifth element. It's the only way."

Alarm bells are clanging through me. "It's not," I whisper. "It doesn't work. In my time, the Knights rise again. *An imperfect solution at best,*" I remind her, as if my grandmother's words will carry weight. But Isobel doesn't even look at me.

Cera's face is troubled. "We have never, never taken our Talents into that realm," she whispers.

"We have never had a need to. *Before,*" Isobel says.

"Let's say we do need this clock, then," Cera begins. "Just how are we going to get it? It's gone. Are you proposing that we just walk in there and ask for it nicely?"

Gabriel shifts, clears his throat. "I've been thinking about that. In our time, Alistair said something about losing it in a card game. What if I Traveled back to an even earlier time and—"

"It won't work," I say instantly. "Liam knows who you are anyway."

Gabriel pauses, raises one eyebrow at me, then continues. "As I just said, I could Travel back *before* this all happened and somehow—"

"No! Don't you see? Liam got you once already. That's how he was able to come to the future, to our time. Don't you remember when he said, 'Don't be angry with your young man. He put up a good fight'?"

Gabriel snorts, but I speak over him. "And please

don't say something stupid about how you could take him in a fight and—"

"Well, it's so obvious, so I don't need to say it—"

"Don't be such an idiot. How much more can you Travel anyway, Gabriel? *You're dying.*"

Gabriel opens his mouth once, then closes it again. He locks his hands together and stares down at them.

"It's not a clock, anyway," Isobel breaks in. "It's a small timepiece. Nothing like a wall clock as far as I can understand. The gift of time freely given. That's what the book said."

"Given freely?" Gabriel interjects. He frowns. "That would have been good to know before we tried to *steal* the damn clock."

But Isobel ignores him. Her gaze sharpens like a knife on me. "And according to the book, you have it."

I blink at her. "Me? I don't have anything like that. I—" I shift in my seat and it's only then that I feel a small pinprick against my thigh.

Jessica's cameo pin. That happens to be a little watch. That she gave me. Freely. Slowly, I reach into my pocket and curl my fingers around the watch. Its steady ticking is like a heartbeat.

Isobel's stare is bright and burning with triumph.

"Okay, so you have the timepiece, but how are you going to get one of the Knights? La Spider and Liam will be on their guard, and—"

"It's not La Spider or Liam," Isobel interjects, stroking Silvius's fur. "It's Jessica. I read that much in the book. *The daughter's blood sacrifice will bind the spell.*"

My fingers clench around the cameo pin. "No. Not Jessica. She's the only one who . . . "

"Who what?" Cera asks curiously. Her face is troubled.

"Who seems to have a heart," I finish, even though I don't know if that's true. She did let Livie die, after all. Still, I try again. "Making Jessica the sacrifice isn't going to work—"

Isobel turns her head. "Enough. We're doing what you wanted us to do."

"But you're not," I say, trying not to let my voice quaver. "This isn't what's supposed to happen at all. Or actually, it *is* what's supposed to happen and then it all unravels somehow in the future."

"Then what's the right answer?" Cera asks quietly, turning to face me.

"It has to be her. And it has to be tomorrow night. Samhain." Isobel's voice is flinty hard. Cera draws in a breath, nods slowly.

"Tomorrow night? How are you going to get Jessica then? You know La Spider won't let her leave the house, and—" My words grind to a halt.

"What is it?" Isobel asks, and the way she turns her face so sharply and regards me with those unblinking eyes makes me shiver. "You know a way to get her out of the house, don't you? Don't you?"

I shake my head.

"You said yourself that he's dying," Isobel explodes suddenly, flinging out one arm toward Gabriel. Silvius whimpers once, sits, then comes to his feet again. He bumps his nose against Isobel's hand, but she ignores him. "We're all going to die soon enough if you don't act. If you know a way to get her out of the house, then say it."

A terrible choice, Thom told me. Either help to kill someone or do nothing and know that everyone you love will die. Glancing once at Gabriel, I realize it's not a choice at all.

"Her music tutor. Before Gabriel. She's in love with him. If you send a message to her saying that he needs to see her, she'll sneak out of the house. She'll come for him."

I close my eyes so I don't have to see the triumph blazing across Isobel's face.

"Nothing yet?"

Gabriel looks at me, the firelight flickering over his wan features.

"I'm sorry," I murmur, lacing my fingers through his. His hand feels cold. "Don't try again."

But he's shaking his head. "It's okay," he whispers. "I just did. Nothing. I still can't find anyone." He closes his eyes again and seems to go into a half-sleeping trance. I swallow, refrain from asking any more questions. I had spent the previous night awake, watching him sleep, reassuring myself that as long as I could hear him still breathing, everything would be okay. That there was still a chance to get him out of this mess alive.

Now I pull my knees in tight to my chest. It's the night of Samhain. A full moon presides over a clear sky filled with thousands of stars. A little over an hour ago, Philben and Phineaus had driven off together in the family carriage to the meeting point where they planned to steal Jessica. I refused to go. Not that anyone had asked me to.

The library door creaks open and Isobel emerges, followed by Cera. The older woman's face is pale, and the lines bracketing her mouth deepen as I stare at her. But it's Isobel who speaks. "The spell is ready. All it needs is the blood of a Knight."

Cera draws in a breath and I steal a sideways glance at her, but she remains silent.

"I'll go ahead," Isobel says to Cera. "To prepare the altar." And she slips away without looking at me. Motioning toward Gabriel, who still has his eyes closed, I rise from the leather chair where I've been sitting and cross the room toward Cera and the fireplace. Fixing my eyes on a bunch of herbs drying over the mantelpiece, I whisper, "Tell me again how this is supposed to work."

Cera sighs, holds out her hands to the blaze, and rubs them together slowly. "You really don't understand spells, do you?"

I shrug. "I wasn't exactly taught them when I was growing up." I had explained as much of my history to her as I was able to.

"Yes, well, I imagine when you and your young man go back, you'll find that all that will have changed."

This is a sidetracking thought, but I let myself go there. Everything will be different. I'll have always known about my Talent. No one will have kept it from me. Maybe I'll never feel the need to escape Hedgerow and go to boarding school in Manhattan. Maybe I'll never get to meet Agatha. Then I shake my head—as of right now, there's nothing to go back to.

"As you do know, our power comes from the elements."

"Earth, Air, Water, Fire," I quote.

"Yes," Cera agrees. "But Blood and Time are also considered elements. Those we rarely touch or call upon. They can be . . . dangerous. They can so easily spiral out of control."

"But the Knights aren't afraid of that."

Her mouth twists downward. "Clearly not." Reaching up, she tugs the bunch of herbs free and begins shredding them between her fingers. A spicy-sweet smell rises from the torn leaves. "If we call all six elements down at once with the blood of one of their own, we think we can . . . change or seal their power away." With a flick of her fingers she tosses some of the leaves into the fire. The flames burn green for a few seconds.

"With the blood of one of their own . . ." I echo softly.

"It has to be," Cera says quietly. "Their blood will bind the spell. Blood calls to blood. Everyone who shares the sacrifice's blood will be affected. Their Talents will be bound up in the Domani and they will never be able to use them again." She hands me a branch of the herb. "Heartsease," she murmurs. "Good for a troubled mind."

Shivering, I trace my finger through the green sap that oozes from the torn leaves. So, they'll be ordinary. Just like . . . Talentless people. Something I've assumed about myself for so many years. Only the Knights wouldn't have years to get used to that reality. They'll have mere seconds. "Would you have done something like this if Thom hadn't died?" I ask.

Cera shrugs, rubbing her fingers down her dress as if to clean them of the sap. "It's not likely," she says at last.

I try to keep my voice even. "Even though they're killing people? People without Talents, but people all the same—"

"I know that," Cera says flatly. "But those people have nothing to do with us."

"But, why? They're still—"

"Listen," Cera says fiercely, snatching another bunch

of herbs to shred into the fire. "Back in the old countries, before we came here, we were followed and persecuted. Sometimes killed for what we had. By those very same *people*. My own great-grandmother was burned at the stake because she could ease anyone's pain and heal most sicknesses. I watched, in a crowd full of those very same people she had cured, as a man dressed all in gray lit the sticks below her feet on fire. And that night we fled. My mother, my brothers, my grandmother and grandfather. My cousins. We had no choice. Except to stay away from those people for the rest of our lives and to make sure our children did as well." She pauses, studies her knotted hands. "And I hope you'll teach your own children the same."

"I don't know about that," I say slowly. "I thought I was one of those *very same people* for so long. My best friend is one of those people. My Aunt Beatrice married someone who wasn't Talented. They're not so bad," I finish, staring down at my green-stained fingers. "Jessica wants to be one of those very same people." I press the little stem of dried leaves to my lips, inhale the scent. It's not working. I think I'd need a bucketful of heartsease.

Cera crosses to the other side of the room and reaches up one hand to unhook another hanging bunch of herbs.

There is a creak of carriage wheels. Gabriel sits upright, his eyes flaring open. "What's going on?" he murmurs thickly.

Cera's face turns toward the window and I follow her

gaze. First Phineaus climbs out of the carriage and then turns, holding open the door. Philben emerges with a body wrapped in a long dark cloak. As he shifts his burden, the cloak falls back. I can see the edge of Jessica's sleeve and her white throat. Philben glances at the sky, then toward the house. His face is inscrutable. Then he and Phineaus turn and head toward the woods, following the path that Isobel took earlier. In just seconds, they are swallowed up by the darkness of the woods.

Shivering, I look away.

Cera regards me for a moment and her face is just as inscrutable as her brother's was a moment earlier. "It will be over quickly," she murmurs, and pressing the rest of the heartsease into my hand, she turns and leaves the room. A minute later, I hear the front door slam.

"Tam?" Gabriel says from the couch.

"They've got her," I say tonelessly. I cross the room again and sink down beside his chair. After a minute, I feel his fingers in my hair.

"There's still time," he says.

"What?"

"To stop this."

I struggle upright and stare at him. His skin is flushed, but his breathing is steady as he says, "We don't have to go through with this. We can go into the woods, grab Jessica, and go back to our time."

I shake my head. "That solves nothing. I can't bring a

Knight into the future. They're determined. And for some reason the book is telling them that it's her. The youngest daughter's sacrifice." I stare into the flames. Sacrifice. *Apparently, you don't understand what it means to sacrifice for your family.*

Bolting upright, I say, "Alistair."

Gabriel's gaze darts to the window as he struggles to sit up. "What? Where?"

"No, sorry. Not here. It's something he said. Something at that Knight dinner about how he saved his family by sacrificing himself." I jump to my feet. "It's not Jessica they need. Or they do, but not just her. I have to go."

"Wait," Gabriel says, coming to his feet. "I'm coming with you."

"No, you can't. You're not . . . Sorry. I know I'm not supposed to tell you what to do."

"Oh, Tamsin," Gabriel says with a beatific smile as he links his arm through mine. I try not to stagger as he leans most of his weight on me. "There's hope for you after all."

I don't have the heart to contradict him.

TWENTY-FOUR

A SHARP WIND IS RISING as we exit the farm-house, making the weathervane horse spin and spin. Clouds have scudded across the moon. Our feet crunch over frozen ridges of earth as we run for the woods. I stumble once in the complete darkness, and Gabriel's hand tightens on mine.

"This way," he says after a second, leading me to an overgrown path that winds into the tangle of trees.

"Please don't let it be too late." I whisper those words over and over as we thrash our way through brambles and low-hanging branches. Finally, up ahead I can see pale ladders of smoke climbing into the sky. They've started the bonfire already.

We took a life. A terrible solution . . . my grandmother's voice cautions.

"*Took* is the operative word here," I mutter to myself, just as the wind, redolent of herbs and pine, slaps me in the face.

We thrash our way through the trees until finally we break into the clearing. Through the flames I can make out the four points of the massive altar on which Jessica is now lying. Isobel stands to the North of the altar with Philben on her left for the East and Phineaus below her to the South. Cera, her face calmly sorrowful, stands at the right of the altar, representing the West. A low chanting rises from the woods and fields that surround the altar. Shadowy forms and faces flicker through the smoke and firelight. The rest of the Greene family has assembled.

Gabriel steps up beside me, puts one hand on my shoulder just as Cera holds her two cupped palms over the altar. A thin stream of dirt trickles from her fingers as she intones in a clear voice, "Earth, rich and deep, nourisher of all, from life to death, calls to the West. Accept our offering."

"Accept our offering," everyone says at once.

Next Isobel sways forward, her face intent. She, too, cups her palms over the altar, then leans down and blows on them once. "Air, giver of breath, invisible to all, from life to death, calls to the North. Accept our offering."

"Accept our offering."

I close my eyes and think back to the last moment I saw my grandmother. I'd sat at her feet in the library. She had sent everyone else out of the room just after she had Rowena consult the book that showed our future as a great empty blank space. *Remember, it's up to you to allow when a*

person's Talent can work on you and when it can't. It's entire-
ly your choice.

Opening my eyes, I watch Isobel step back, gracefully giving way to Philben. He stretches his palms above the
altar and fire licks from his skin to light the four candles
placed on the stone slab. "Fire, bright and hot, giver of light,
from life to death, calls to the East. Accept our offering."

As everyone repeats these last words, Jessica's eyes
flicker open. Her head twists to the left and then the right
and then her mouth drops open in terror. Through the rising wind and the chanting, I can't hear what she's saying,
but I can only imagine it.

Phineaus moves forward, holding a small gold chalice.
I close my eyes.

"Water, sweet and pure, washing away all sorrows,
calls to the South. Accept our offering." He tips the chalice
forward and anoints the South of the altar with the contents
of the cup.

"Accept our offering," all of them echo. They step
forward.

Jessica's throat, bare to the moonlight, moves once as
if she's swallowing her screams, and her eyes gaze upward
as if she's begging for help from the sky above.

A terrible choice, my grandmother's voice whispers
once again to me, and suddenly instead of these nineteenth-
century Greenes I can see the ghostly shadows of my family
standing around the circle of fire. My mother is smiling up

[257]

at my father and Rowena is laughing, her face bright with happiness, while all my uncles and aunts crowd in, clapping their hands and turning this way and that, swaying a little in the dark as if they're dancing. And I can see my grandmother, her face glimmering faintly in the moonlight.

"It's not even a choice," I whisper back to her ghost shadow. "Not a choice at all," I add as Gabriel's hand tightens on my shoulder.

I blink once and my shadow family vanishes. Thunder shakes the sky above me, and the rain sheets down. Wind is pouring through the clearing, whipping the flames higher and higher. Cera, with a face of stone, pulls a curved silver knife from her belt. She holds her other hand above Jessica's heart and the firelight catches on the little cameo watch hanging on a fine silver chain.

Cera lifts the knife to the sky, crying out, "Oh, four elements and four directions, guide this knife truly and accept our plea." Lightning cracks, then seems to liquefy and pour directly into her hand, burnishing the blade. With a plunging motion, she thrusts the knife downward.

In that same second, I gather myself and dissolve into Jessica's body. I have the strangest sensation of floating in a sun-warmed lake and then I blink and open my eyes, watching the knife descend like a shard of light.

"Accept my offering," I whisper, just as Cera's voice says, "And this blood spilled will seal the spell."

I close my eyes again, feeling an icicle where my heart

used to be. Now I have the sensation of falling through darkening layers of water as I spread myself through Jessica's body, shielding her spirit with my own. *This is my choice, my choice, my choice. I allow this,* I whisper to us both. With the final shreds of strength, I turn Jessica's head to stare at the cameo watch face.

In a blur of blood-red color, the watch hands begin spinning as lightning splinters down again, forming a cage of sparks over the altar. When the hour hand points to one degree east of a new day, I push Jessica's hand against her heart, willing it to heal. Only when her skin fuses together do I wrench myself free of Jessica's body to lie huddled next to her on the cold stone slab. Rain beats down on us both and I have one glimpse of Cera's horrified face before I turn my head back to Jessica. Her eyes are locked on mine, her lips trembling slightly as my blood continues to pour from my chest. A slow soft ticking fills my ears, little miniature chimes of the hour.

"Why?" she whispers.

Or maybe it's my heart beating its last beats as my blood and Jessica's blood seals the Domani.

I form the words slowly in my head, force them to my lips in time with the doleful ringing of bells that is now clanging inside my head. Five, six, seven. "It was the right thing," I whisper.

Her eyes travel downward to where I know my life is spilling away.

I allow this, I allow this, I allow this, I whisper in my mind, watching her blood and mine mingle.

The clock chimes nine. Quick as thought, Jessica presses her hand over my heart. Blood bubbles up through her fingers. Ten, eleven.

"For once, for once in my life I will use it for when I want to, not for when someone else tells me to . . . " she whispers.

On the twelfth chime her hand slips away and the edges of her face blur and dissolve into darkness.

TWENTY-FIVE

SOFTNESS. WARMTH. FEATHERS.

Feathers?

Yes, feathers. Tickling my nose.

"Acch-hooo!!" I come to life with a tremendous sneeze. My eyes fly open and I'm confronted with the flat yellow gaze of one of Isobel's ravens. It flaps its wings, resettles itself on the table next to the bed I'm lying in. Jerking its black head left and right, it lets out a sharp caw. And then another for good measure.

"Tamsin?" My gaze swivels downward to where Gabriel is half sitting in a chair and half lying across the foot of the bed. He pushes up on his elbows, blinks his eyes at me once. "You're alive."

I raise one eyebrow. "I see that you were so concerned that you fell asleep over me." The second the words leave my mouth, I'm sorry. The skin around his eyes has taken on a bruised look, and his hands are trembling as he clasps them together. But Gabriel only gives me that long, even look I've come to expect from him and moves closer up the bed to me while I fight my way free of the feather comforter, and then he's holding me so tightly that I can draw only the thinnest of breaths into my lungs.

"Did it work?"

He releases me and nods once. "It did." Then he begins pleating the edge of the coverlet between his fingers.

Someone has to say it. "It's gone, isn't it?" I whisper. "My Talent."

And suddenly tears are burning at the backs of my eyelids and I bring my hands up to my face and start to cry in huge, shuddering gasps.

It worked the way I had hoped.

And the way I had dreaded, too.

"It's in the Domani?" I ask, even though I know the answer.

Gabriel nods again. "It's shielding all of the Knights' power. You . . . did it, Tamsin. You found a way to make sure that none of the Knights would ever be able to take it back again."

I lift my head and look at him, tears still dripping from my chin. On the bedside table, the raven hops a few steps closer, cocking its head, studying me.

"So it worked? With Jessica's blood in there, too?"

"Enough of that got in there, too. When you went inside of her, your blood joined with hers."

I shake my head in wonder and then pull open my

shirt. The faintest of lines crisscrosses the skin over my heart. "She healed me, though? She used her Talent."

"It was the last time she could. The clock," he says, and I think back to the moments that are now swirled in my head.

"Before it struck twelve," I say. "She healed me."

Gabriel nods. "So you see, Tam? It's not gone, your Talent. It'll always be there in the Domani from now until . . . forever."

I nod, knowing there's no way to explain the despair that floods through me. Even though I had hoped for this, even though technically I've known that I had a Talent for only a few short months, the loss of it leaves me hollow inside. Now, staring up at the wooden beamed ceiling at the bunches of dried lavender and roses hanging from the rafters, I contemplate how nothing will ever be the same again.

Gabriel reaches for my hands, but just then the door creaks open. Isobel and Cera enter the room.

The raven squawks, flaps its wings, and circles the room twice. Cera waves her hand in the air, an irritated expression crossing her face as the raven swoops past her head to land on Isobel's shoulder.

"Awake and well?" Cera asks me. I nod. "Any pain?"

Just my heart. It feels like it's missing.

"No," I say softly, aware that Isobel is studying me. She digs one booted foot into the floor.

"Tamsin," she says softly. "I . . . what you did . . . for us. After everything . . ." She bows her head. "I'm sorry," she whispers.

"If you don't mind," Cera begins. "I'd like a word with Tamsin. Alone."

Gabriel looks at me. I shrug, so he pulls himself from the chair and he and Isobel move toward the door, shutting it softly behind them.

I turn my head and stare out the small diamond-paned window. The sky is a brilliant clear pink in the east, and the last of the stars are fading. All traces of the storm clouds seem to have blown themselves out.

The chair creaks softly as Cera settles her weight into it. I turn my head against the pillow, inhaling the scent of lavender and pine and something else I can't identify. "That was a brave thing you did, Tamsin," she says quietly, her hands clasped together in her lap. "A very brave thing."

I shrug again, but fresh tears begin leaking from the corner of my eyes.

"A thing that no one else in our family would ever think to do. You willingly gave up your Talent to save us all. I wouldn't have done it. Isobel wouldn't have—"

"You couldn't," I whisper. "It wasn't in the nature of your Talent. Mine was always . . . different. My grandmother told me that it was my choice to allow spells or other people's Talents to work on me. So it's not that I—"

But Cera holds up her hand. "No. You made a choice

that no one else would have been brave enough to make. Your name will be remembered."

At this I sit up a little farther. "I don't want it to."

Cera frowns at me. "And why not?"

"Because," I say, scrubbing the backs of my hands against my eyes. "I don't want people's pity."

"*Pity?* I hardly—"

"I don't want people to whisper about me any more than they already do, already did before I . . . before I knew that I had a Talent. I can handle not having a Talent. I just don't want people to know that I used to." I clench my hands around the covers. It occurs to me that there's one other person who might be feeling something of what I'm feeling.

"I'd like to see Jessica Knight."

Cera hesitates.

"She's alive, right?" I say, suddenly alarmed.

"Of course," Cera says. "She's in the next room. And I think she'd like to see you, too."

I rustle back the bedcovers and place my feet on the floor, feeling the cool wood beneath my toes. I am surprisingly steady on my feet and shake my head at Cera's offer of her arm. As I follow her to the door, my mind churns with the last images of Jessica Knight and what she must be thinking now.

We pass into the narrow, empty hallway and Cera leads me to the door next to mine. "Is she—"

But Cera gives me a little push, and so I knock on the door. After Jessica's "Come in," I turn the knob and enter the room. It's small and narrow, similar in length and proportion to mine. As to be expected, Jessica is not lying in bed. Instead, she is fully dressed in clothes that either Cera or Isobel must have given her, standing with her back to the door, staring out the window. At the sound of my slow footsteps, she turns and opens her mouth, then seems to choke on whatever it was she was going to say. She takes a few steps forward, her face pale in the lamplight, her hair hanging loosely down her back.

"Are you in pain?" I ask her, feeling that this is probably a stupid question. What else would she be in? She just lost her Talent forever. Like me.

Jessica touches the tips of her fingers to her heart. She shakes her head. "No. You took care of that. Are you?"

"No." Then I echo, "You took care of that."

She regards me for a moment without speaking. "Why did you do it, Tamsin?"

And even though I know she knows my real name now, it's still something of a shock to hear her say it. "Which part?"

She flushes a dull red. "Why did you save me?"

I look at the lamp until my eyes ache. "Because you didn't seem like the rest of your family."

When I look back, small orbs of light burst across my

vision. "Neither are you," Jessica says slowly. "For once in my life I used my Talent for something . . . for something that I wanted to use it for. Not for what my mother or my brother told me to do."

"Is that why you wouldn't save Livie?" I ask, my throat suddenly dry, afraid of her answer.

She blinks at me. "I *did* save Livie. Over and over again. At my brother and my mother's insistence. Only the last time, she . . . she looked at me and she begged me to let her die." Jessica draws in a breath. "So, I did." She pauses, touches her throat, and suddenly I realize her fingers are unconsciously seeking her missing cameo pin. The one that's been turned into the new Domani now. But Jessica is still speaking, so I let that thought go. "I'm glad it's gone. I feel . . . lighter. I feel free." She is silent for a moment as if waiting for a response, and then when I can't find anything to say, she continues. "I take it you don't feel quite the way I feel."

I shrug. "What will you do now?"

Jessica smiles at me, a full real smile. "I intend to live," she says quietly. "I suggest you do the same."

Jessica, Gabriel, and I stand in silence across the street from the Knights' house, staring at the shattered windowpanes on either side of the front door. Although the street bustles with the usual amount of afternoon traffic, the house seems frozen and still. I have an eerie sense of having been here before. Then it hits me. This is a reverse echo of my grandmother's vision of what could have happened to my family's house in Hedgerow.

"Are they in there?" Jessica asks finally, glancing at us.

Gabriel nods. "Every last one of them."

Then he pauses. "Except for Alistair."

I draw in a shuddering breath. "What do you mean?"

"I can't find him at all." He glances down at me. "He's dead, Tamsin. His body's there, but he's not anymore."

A horse-drawn carriage clips past us, temporarily obscuring my view of the Knights' house. Wrapping my arms around myself, I digest Gabriel's words for a minute. I would have thought this news would come as a relief, but I actually feel numb. "And the rest of the Knights?" I finally ask. "Their Talents?"

Gabriel nods again. "Also gone. All of it." He touches his hand to his temple and I step closer to him.

"How can you be sure?" Jessica asks, giving him a curious glance.

"Because it's the thing that they all desire the most. It's coming out of the house like a tidal wave," he says quietly.

I turn to her. "You don't need to go in there," I say. "I—"

"I'm not afraid of them anymore," she says quietly. "They can't hurt me now."

I arch an eyebrow. "I don't know. La Spider seems pretty handy with a gun."

Jessica's forehead wrinkles slightly. "La Spider? . . . Oh." One hand flashes up to her mouth to conceal a smile. "My mother." She nods, considering.

"William Finnegan will be glad to see you no matter what," I say softly.

For a long moment, Jessica stares at the broken shell of her family's house. Then she nods, brushes her hands down the skirt of her borrowed dress. "That's true," she says, and her smile breaks free again, lighting her face in a way that makes her almost pretty. She looks at Gabriel and me for a long moment and then says simply, "Goodbye," before turning away and walking down the street.

I wait until she has turned the corner and disappeared for good before saying, "Can you get us home? Is there a home?"

He nods.

"Is it still in Hedgerow?"

"Afraid so, Tam."

I sigh. "Couldn't that have at least changed?"

"Are you sure you don't want to go visit Coney Island while we're here? Walk across the Brooklyn Bridge or something?" Gabriel asks, smiling down at me.

"You're on borrowed time, Gabriel." Then I stop and consider something. So am I, at this moment. And all at once the pain of losing my Talent floods through me again. Blinking back tears, I say lightly enough, "Besides, has the Brooklyn Bridge even been built yet?"

Gabriel rolls his eyes. "Your lack of knowledge about the city you live in is embarrassing. It was built in 1883." Then he grins at me. "I studied up on a lot of nineteenth-century New York facts. I had to do something while I was waiting for you to let me find you."

Sunlight edges across the cobblestones. "Yeah, well. Guess I won't be stopping you from doing that anymore."

"Tam," Gabriel says, but I shake my head.

"Forget it. I'm ready."

He looks like he wants to say more, but he takes my outstretched hands in his and looks inward. I curl my toes in my too-big boots—at last I can wear some other shoes—and turn my face away from the Knight House, up to the sky. I keep my eyes wide open. Who knows if I'll ever see any of this again. Colors swoop in and out of the darkness surrounding me, and I hear my grandmother's voice. *Your daughter will be one of the most powerful we have ever seen in this family. She will be a beacon for us all.*

And then we are standing in a familiar driveway staring up at the outlines of my family's house in Hedgerow. Light is blazing from every window and the sound of voices and laughter reaches my ears. Snowflakes drift lazily through the air, the kind that are round and fat and melt so fast.

"You did it," I say to Gabriel, giving his hands a quick squeeze before letting go.

"You doubted me?" he answers, one eyebrow arched.

"Well . . ."

"Come on," he says.

But I can't make my feet move. After a second he turns, his arms swinging a little with the motion. "I can't," I whisper. "I'm . . ." I turn my face skyward, letting the snowflakes land on my cheeks and eyelashes, taking deep breaths of the frost-tinged air. "I'm not me," I finish.

And then Gabriel is holding me by the shoulders, forcing me to look at him.

"You're exactly you. No, don't shake your head, listen to me," he says, flexing his fingers on my shoulders. "My Talent doesn't make me who I am. Your Talent didn't make you who you are. You're the same person you've been all along. What you did last night, for your family, no one else would have done. That's *you*, Tamsin. *That's who you are.*"

I consider this for a moment. Then, not trusting myself to speak, I nod.

Gabriel pauses, then continues with, "And I love you. I know that doesn't fix anything you're feeling right now, I know that doesn't help, but—"

"It doesn't hurt," I interject, pleased that my voice only cracks a little at the end.

He smiles, cradles my face with his two hands, and kisses me as the snowflakes fall gently all around us.

At last we pull apart. I take a deep breath and say, "We changed so many things in the past, Gabriel. What if everything's so different now?"

"Only one way to find out."

I nod. "I know. Let's go in."

Hand in hand, we climb the hill of the driveway toward the house.

EPILOGUE

CLOMPING UP THE PORCH, I reach out for the screen door only to have it flung open from the inside. Rowena is standing just inside the doorway, the light shining through her hair. "Finally," she cries gaily, and flings her arms around me.

"Ooof," I mutter in response, but she doesn't seem to notice. Instead, she pulls both of us indoors into the crowded kitchen. It seems that all my family is packed inside, spilling in and out of rooms. Everyone seems to be talking at once, laughing and shouting, but before I can focus on any one thing, Rowena is babbling away in my ear.

"Oh, Agatha called. She said she couldn't get you on your cell. She's coming up tomorrow on the ten a.m. train, not the eleven, so we have to remember to get her at the station, and also, you got a letter from Stanford that is very, *very* thick." She gives my hand a little squeeze. "I think this could be it, Tam. Aren't you excited? You got into *Stanford!*

It's what you always wanted!" She's smiling so genuinely at me that I can't help but frown. Luckily, she doesn't seem to notice as she babbles on. "Oh, and I want you to tell me what you think of—"

"What?" I manage to say. "Wait a minute. Agatha's coming here? Stanford?"

My sister gives me a quizzical look. "Yes. She's coming for my wedding. Remember, we invited her last month?" She leads me through the living room, where more of my relatives are clustered.

"Ah, the city girl is back," Uncle Morris says, popping into the air next to me. I jump a little.

"Tamsin," Uncle Chester calls from the corner, where he is juggling pieces of a broken plate through the air. My mother looks up from the couch, smiling at me, before narrowing her eyes at Uncle Chester.

"Okay," I murmur, trying to steady myself against this onslaught of information. "I need a minute here," I mutter to Gabriel. Before anyone can say anything else, I slip out the side door into the backyard.

Where it was snowing just a few minutes ago, a soft breeze scented with jasmine is now blowing and the air feels practically balmy. In spite of everything, I smile and look toward the greenhouse, where one light shines. Typical of my father to call up spring in the middle of December. I wander past my family's altar, which is bedecked with red and gold leaves and a basket of apples and sweet herbs.

The apples are so deeply scarlet that they're almost glowing in the moonlight. And then my feet take me a little farther out into the meadow and I'm drawn to a simple stone marker adorned with a wreath of dried purple flowers. Crouching down, I gently push the wreath aside to read the engraved words: THOM GREENE.

"They came here in 1899. Isobel and Cera, Philben and Phineaus. A few of us stayed in the city and bought the house on Washington Square that you well know. But those four wanted the peace of the countryside, where they could live unhindered."

Turning my head, I regard my grandmother, who has come to stand beside me. Her breathing is light and shallow, but the moonlight is kind to her, smoothing out the wrinkles from her face until she almost seems like a young girl again. Like the girl I met in another garden in 1939. Her eyes shine at me. "Well done, Tamsin. No one else could have accomplished it."

Shrugging, I clamber to my feet. There are a hundred things I could say, but I say the only one. "It's really gone, isn't it?"

My heart beats painfully in my chest until my grandmother bows her head and says one word. "Yes."

I draw in one breath, then another as a sudden realization floods through me. At last I understand why my grandmother raised me the way she did. For seventeen years she let me think that I didn't have a Talent so I would understand just how to live now that it's truly gone. I press my hands to my eyes. "But what am I now?" I ask her, my voice a thin thread under the star-filled sky. "I'm not a witch now. And I'm not an ordinary person? Am I?"

My grandmother is watching me steadily. Slowly she takes my hand. "You are a beacon for us. One of the most powerful."

"I'm not," I say softly. "Not anymore."

Smiling, my grandmother presses my hand. "Always, Tamsin. Because of you, we have a future. That's why you will *always* be a beacon for us." Still holding my hand, she turns toward the house, toward the sound of laughter and music spilling out from the lit windows.

Looking back at her, I smile, close my eye in her trademark wink, and say, "Ah."